The Most Boring Book Ever Written

An adventure-less pick-your-path[*] novella

Rudolf Kerkhoven

&

Daniel Pitts

---

[*] Not to be confused with a choose-your-own-adventure novel. Very different.

OTHER BOOKS BY RUDOLF KERKHOVEN & DANIEL PITTS

The Adventures of Whatley Tupper (A pick-your-path novel)

The Redemption of Mr. Sturlubok (A pick-your-path novel)

Can Stuart Henry Zhang Save the World? (A pick-your-path novel)

OTHER BOOKS BY RUDOLF KERKHOVEN

The Year We Finally Solved Everything

A Dream Apart

Love is not free. The price is 99 cents.

How the Worlds Ends (Book One) (2017)

How the World Ends (Book Two) (2018)

How the World Ends (Book Three) (2018)

IF YOU ENJOY THIS BOOK (WOULDN'T THAT BE IRONIC?) PLEASE REVIEW IT AT AMAZON.COM. IT HELPS.

Ann is your wife
Emma is your daughter
That is **it.**

■　■　■

You were once one of the elite—among the most skilled and respected (if not feared) fighter pilots in the American air force. The F-22 Raptor, F-177 Nighthawk and even the F-35 Lightning II—all of these jets were at one time under your expert control. Serving your country in Afghanistan, Kosovo, and both Iraqi wars, your call sign was *Ace of Spades*, the highest ranked card, and the reason was simple: you were the best of the best.

But now you're forty and those heady days are long behind you. Married with a four year-old daughter, you work as a commercial pilot for a mid-sized airline that specializes in short-haul flights across the American mid-west. You live in a comfortable three-bedroom home (with an unfinished basement that could easily incorporate a fourth) in a quiet and safe suburban community only thirty minutes from the airport, which is not too bad, you have to admit. You know a lot of people who spend forty-five minutes, if not *an hour,* driving to work each way.

All in all, your life is pretty darn good.

This particular morning you are briskly awoken from your dream (in which you were installing oak flooring in that unfinished basement) by the grating alarm clock just to your right. Instinctively you reach for the large and punchable snooze button… but then wonder if you should just flick off the alarm and start your day right now?

■ **What do you do?** ■

Turn to page 4 if you hit the snooze button.

Turn to page 5 if you turn off the alarm.

Sure, you bought yourself nine more minutes, or 540 seconds as you liked to think of it, but afterwards you feel no more refreshed. It was a waste of time, which means it was a waste of your life. It's decided then: tomorrow you'll just turn it off. No more snoozing. You've made this decision before, of course. In fact, you make this decision essentially each and every morning in which you're awoken by the alarm. But today, you feel more assured in yourself. Today, you know that you'll do something different tomorrow.

You look over to Ann, her mouth open as wide as a jet hanger with crusted drool on either side of her lips. After scratching your groin with a couple of quick paws of your right hand, you slip out of bed, crack your neck, and then saunter into the ensuite bathroom, flicking on the lights as you stumble to the sink to grab your toothbrush.

Lifting the brush towards your face, you observe the overused bristles, limp and flaccid, sinking into a sad V-formation from semi-daily use. How many days now have you meant to get a new toothbrush? And yet, here you are, once again inspecting the beleaguered instrument. You pull it close and contemplate the number of weary bristles before your weary eyes. Hundreds? Thousands? Even if there were a million, would they still be able to perform their job dutifully? In the military, you received a fresh toothbrush every week from the supply depot. Some believed polished shoes were important, but for you, it's your teeth.

Didn't you brush yesterday with the same brush and you survived? Your teeth were cleaned, weren't they? What did it matter? Some people never brushed and they were still perfectly adequate citizens. Or were they?

What type of man worries about such things?

You do.

■ What do you do? ■

Turn to page 21 if you use your wife's pink brush.

Turn to page 23 if you use your own, just brush a little longer than normal.

No. Although always tempting to partake in a few more minutes of rest, it isn't needed. Really, what difference would nine additional minutes make after eight hours of joyful rest? An extra 2% of sleep, that's what. *2%*. When was the last time you became excited over an extra 2% of anything? Okay—there was that time you purchased several gallons of 2% milk when it was buy-one-get-one-free. That was moderately exciting. But this was different. It wasn't buy-one-get-2%-free.

Anyhow.

You flick off the alarm and sit up with a grateful stretch.

Giving Ann a quick kiss on the cheek (to which she moans and rolls over), you then trundle to the ensuite bathroom and twist on the shower. After thirty impatient and chilled seconds, you step into the torrent of warm water, eyes closed, head down, shoulders slack. It feels fantastic here, as refreshing as an ice cold glass of 7-UP on a hot summer's day. You wish that this could last forever.

And then you have a crazy thought.

■ What do you do? ■

Turn to page 6 if you decide to plug the drain and take a relaxing 9-minute bath (seeing as you didn't hit the snooze button.)

Turn to page 8 if you lather up and get on with the rest of your morning routines.

It's like when the airline stewards offer you a snack pack of oatmeal raisin cookies right after you've finished your lunch. You're not hungry. You don't need it. You're perfectly fine as it is. But you can't help yourself. It's just too tempting.

You plug the drain and lie back against the cool porcelain bathtub. You close your eyes, listening to the rushing water, feeling the warmth creep up your legs, chest, and arms. Soon the water tickles your chin and you twist the tap shut with your right foot.

There's something soothing about the quietly whirring fan, the rhythmic droplets of water, the lapping and trickling waves… and soon you slip back into a dream…

You're standing in your kitchen, sorting through the recycling while Ann cuts celery beside you. You grab an empty jar of pasta sauce from under the sink and place it into the blue bag for containers. You withdraw an empty box of cornflakes and fold it up before sliding it into the grey bag for paper products. You find an empty can of 7-UP and rinse it out under the tap before dropping it into the blue bag. You then pull out an odd glass jar, curved like a vase and without any markings or labels at all. What was this for? Can it be recycled? You could ask Ann. She's standing right beside you. She must know what this is. But you just shrug your shoulders and drop it into the bag with the other containers.

Looking up towards the television, you're drawn to a peculiar car commercial. There's something familiar about the man giving the pitch and you lean forward. And then it hits you: it's Scott Bakula of *Quantum Leap* fame. You laugh and look over to Ann: "Hey look, Scott Bakula is selling cars now!"

…There is a knocking at the door and you open your eyes, back in your bathtub. Ann pushes the door open a few inches and speaks in a whisper. "Are you okay?"

"Yeah, just decided to take a bath."

"It was so quiet in here, I wasn't sure."

"No, I'm fine." You sit up, still remembering that zany and vivid dream, wondering if Ann would be interested in listening to your recollection of it.

■ What do you do? ■

Turn to page 18 if you decide to tell Ann about the Scott Bakula dream.

Turn to page 20 if you decide to keep it to yourself and get ready.

Really, where were these impulsive thoughts coming from? You surely didn't become one of the most respected pilots in the world by opting for morning snoozes or taking weekday baths. Every minute of the day is precious and you quickly and efficiently clean yourself in the shower, not even pondering the idea of wasting any more time.

Descending the stairs wrapped in a fine white Egyptian cotton towel, you are greeted by the smell of fresh coffee and Ann in the kitchen, pouring a couple of cups.

"Thanks," you say, accepting the ceramic mug while opening the fridge. "Hey, do we have any milk left?"

"Yeah, I'm pretty sure," Ann says with a tinge of annoyance; you know that she assumes you haven't searched thoroughly and want her to find it for you. And you know this because it's true. But you look a little harder before saying anything more, inspecting the door of the stuffed fridge, your eyes continually getting caught on a quart of buttermilk.

"No, I don't see it," you finally reply, now certain that you've searched everywhere.

"I'm sure we have some."

"All I see is the buttermilk."

"Really?" Ann finally comes to the fridge and nudges you out of the way. She looks through the door and slides around various condiments and jars on the top two shelves. "I could swear we had some milk."

"I would have thought so to, but I looked pretty hard."

She sighs and then moans. "Ah, I remember. I made—"

"—That smoothie last night," you quickly finish her sentence. "After yoga."

She nods with an apologetic smile on her face while closing the fridge door. "Yeah, I guess I should have picked up some milk last night on the way home from the gym."

"That's okay."

"I'm sorry."

"No, that's fine. I used to drink it black all the time. Do you want me to pick up some milk on the way home from work today?"

She thinks about this for only a moment before nodding in agreement. "Yeah, if you don't mind." But then she shakes her head. "Actually, I'll be done work today before you. Don't worry about it. I'll get it."

■ What do you do? ■

Turn to page 10 if you insist on going to the store after work.

Turn to page 12 if you agree to let your wife pick up the milk herself.

You know that she is merely being polite. It doesn't make sense for her to go to the supermarket after work. "Thanks, but I'll get it. You'll be busy."

"I'll still be done work before you."

"But you'll be with Emma."

"Oh, she'll be fine. No, seriously," Ann shakes her head, "It's fine. I was the one who finished it."

"Yeah, but that doesn't matter. Just leave it to me. I got it."

She's adamant: "But I'll have to pick up a few things for dinner anyhow after work. Don't worry about it."

You sigh, still thinking it's unfair for her—although she seems quite insistent this morning.

■ **What do you do?** ■

Turn to page 12 if you accept her offer to pick up the milk.

Turn to page 11 if you continue to insist on picking up the milk.

You shake your head with a smile, "I'm going to the store. That's final."

Ann laughs, "No, it's not final. I've got it."

"I insist. I'll pick up the milk."

"No you won't. Like I said, I have other stuff to pick up. It just makes sense. Now, don't you have to go upstairs and get dressed?"

You can tell that she's not going to let up. Perhaps it would be for the best for her to do the shopping?

Turn to page 12.

You nod, accepting her offer. "Okay, then." You feel like there should be something else to say, as if this conversation is lacking a suitable conclusion. And yet there is nothing else to say. You sip from your coffee again and nod. "That would be good."

"Sure."

"And maybe pick up some 7-UP, as well."

"Okay."

You take another slurping sip and look around the kitchen. "That would be great."

Ann just nods and you suspect that she isn't listening. So you nod a few more times and mutter something about getting dressed before ascending the stairs to your bedroom.

Looking through your closet, you accept that there really aren't many wardrobe choices for a pilot. Black slacks. White dress shirt. Black blazer with brass buttons and a few gold stripes. The only avenue for self-expression in a pilot's wardrobe comes from his tie—and you finger through the long line of neatly organized accessories, unsure of what you want today, what would best relay your mood and character to the world. You certainly have a wide variety of choices: charcoal, pewter, silver, slate, steel, leaden, shadow, newsprint, dark gray, light gray… and just gray.

After much deliberation, you select two. But there can only be one.

Sometimes it seems that life would be so much easier *without* all these options…

■ **What do you do?** ■

Turn to page 13 if you go with the charcoal tie.

Turn to page 14 if you go with the dark gray tie.

Today, you feel a little spicy—and nothing says spicy like the color charcoal. Or is it even a color? You recall from grade school being informed that shades of gray do not count as colors. Why is this? How can brown be a color but not charcoal? No, damn it—you're not going to be constrained by the arbitrary constructs of the past. And what did Mrs. Parsons know, anyhow? Didn't' she say that Canada was the second largest country in the world? Preposterous. It's decided then: charcoal is now a color. You quickly get dressed, pleased with your *color* choice as you stand in front of the mirror, finalizing the ensemble with the short-rimmed black captain's hat.

Just before leaving, you pop into Emma's room, careful not to wake her as you kiss her on the cheek and leave. You wave goodbye to Ann as she checks her email and hurry down into the dark and cavernous garage. Punching the illuminated plastic button, you wait for something to happen.

But nothing happens.

The garage door doesn't open.

You sigh and press the button again—bemoaning the time and hassle that will surely be required later this evening to remedy the problem.

But the garage door opens this time. You must have just not pressed the button hard enough the first time. That was close.

As the door lifts and bathes the garage in the bright light of morning, your eyes immediately gloss over your own black Volvo sedan towards the gleaming chrome Jaguar XKR just to its side. It isn't yours, of course. The Jaguar belongs to your old military friend Carlos who asked you to take care of it while on operation overseas. It is a beautiful car—sleek, modern, expensive, and entirely impractical. You shake your head for a moment, wondering why Carlos would spend his money on such a trophy car... but then figure that he'd never know if you took it out for a spin. Really, what was stopping you from driving his Jaguar to work today?

◼ What do you do? ◼

Turn to page 16 if you decide to take Carlos's Jaguar to work today.

Turn to page 17 if you decide to take your own Volvo, as usual.

Dark gray it is. Charcoal is a little too outlandish—people would think that you were desperate for attention. And desperation is certainly not a trait that passengers or stewards desire in their leader. You know of a pilot for a rival airline who always wears a bowtie, naively assuming it adds flair to his image. Shaking your head in dismay, you struggle to recall his name as your wife enters the bedroom. "Ann, what is the name of the pilot who wears a bowtie?"

"Don't know," she yells back from the ensuite.

"Are you sure?"

"I would remember meeting a guy like that."

"You never actually met him."

"Then how would I have known him?"

"I'm sure I joked about him."

"Why?"

"Because he wears a bowtie."

"Is that funny?"

"It's ridiculous."

"Are you going to see him today?"

"Of course not. He's a fool. He wears a bowtie."

Ann doesn't respond which means that either the conversation is over or that she has left the room. Sadly, there is nothing more you can do to recall the bowtie-wearing pilot's name. Not even Google will help you with this. Amazing, that in this day and age that you are forced to just give up.

Shrugging your shoulders, you look at the time and realize that it's time to go. You pop on your short-rimmed black hat and position it just perfectly in the mirror. It cannot be denied: you look good. It comes as no surprise that you did so well with the ladies before settling down with Ann. There were those crazy nights in Mexico, in Greece, in Florida, in Hawaii, in San Diego, in Japan, in Budapest, in Turkey, in—

"Daddy? What's bowtie?"

Your more lurid thoughts are cast aside upon seeing your daughter Emma standing at the opening of your walk-in closet, rubbing her eyes awake.

■ What do you do? ■

Turn to page 78 if you tell her that it's nothing and give her a kiss goodbye.

Turn to page 79 if you attempt to describe what a bowtie is to your four year-old daughter.

Hanging from a hook on the wall are the keys to the Jaguar and you reach out to clasp them. The sleek and powerful car sparkles under the early morning sunlight like a freshly poured glass of 7-UP. But then you let go. It wouldn't be right. Carlos trusted you to keep his car safe for a simple reason: you are his most responsible friend. Maybe in your twenties you would have given in to such impulsive and shortsighted thoughts, but not now.

You grab the keys to the Volvo and descend the steps towards your car.

Turn to page 17.

Would a Jaguar meet the five-star safety requirements you need to feel secure on the road? Absolutely not. Safety is paramount in the life of a domestic pilot and driving on the roads is fraught with peril. If only obtaining a driver's license was as difficult as getting a pilot's license, then perhaps you'd change your mind and take the Jaguar. But until then...

You slide into your fine Swedish automobile and pat the dash gently, caressing the smooth plastic while muttering words of encouragement to your sweet-if-homely ride. The vehicle starts easily and you slide the gearbox into reverse, checking the rearview mirror three times before easing out of the garage and onto the driveway. It's tight and for the hundredth time you yearn for flagmen to ease you out. Under the bright morning sun—the sky's as clear as a glass of 7-UP soda—you reach down and slip on a pair of aviator sunglasses with fine brass frames and lenses as dark as that Latin women you met more than ten years ago during a wild night in Tijuana. She went by the name *Caliente* and definitely lived up to her moniker. It was the time you performed the double hat trick. She was amazing. You were amazing.

But that was then. Now at your age such a sexual feat would cause far too much chaffing to be even remotely pleasurable. And surely that can't be good for a man's prostate? But these thoughts disappear when you turn your head and spot your neighbor, Roger Wang, mowing his front lawn. He looks up expectantly.

■ **What do you do?** ■

Turn to page 24 if you give him a nonchalant head-nod.

Turn to page 25 if you give him a thumbs-up.

Just before Ann can close the door, you sit up a few inches and add: "Actually, I had this really weird dream just now."

"Oh yeah," she says while scratching something that looks like dried milk from the corner of her eye.

"Yeah. In the dream I was sorting through the recycling in the kitchen and you were cutting celery beside me. There was this strange glass container and I couldn't figure out what it was from or if it could even be recycled."

"Huh."

"Yeah, and I was watching a commercial where Scott Bakula was selling cars."

Ann cocks her head, "Was he the weird guy from the prenatal class? The one with the sideburns and earrings?"

"No, no, no. Scott *Bakula*," you emphasize his surname, assuming that Ann didn't hear you properly the first time. "You know." You nod, expecting some look of acknowledgement from your wife. It's obvious. "Scott Bakula."

"Who's that?"

"From *Quantum Leap*?"

She grimaces apologetically. "Was that a code name for one of your operations in Iraq?"

"No, the television show. The guy who travelled in time."

Ann clearly doesn't have a clue. "I guess I never saw it. But, what else happened?"

"Well, he would become transported into people's bodies, do something good in their lives and then travel to a different person in another point in time."

"That's what happened in your dream?"

"No, in *Quantum Leap*."

"But what about the dream?"

"Oh, he was just selling cars."

"That's it?"

"Yeah. It seemed weird. Why would Scott Bakula stoop to selling cars in cheap commercials? He's Scott Bakula!"

"Oh yeah." Ann fakes a laugh and nods. "Okay, then. I'll let you finish getting ready."

She gently closes the door and you're left wondering about how your wife could never have heard of *Quantum Leap*. Was she really that much younger? Perhaps you could find old episodes on DVD somewhere… or maybe on Netflix? You make a mental note of keeping an eye out for the show, wishing there was a way to make a literal note while naked and in the bath. Perhaps some sort of washable crayon and slate? It seems like a good idea—you really did seem to come up with some of your better ideas while soaking in the tub. You then make a mental note to make an actual note about this bath-time note-taking device that (if not already invented) could become quite the big-seller.

Noticing the time, you realize that you need to quit your daydreaming and get ready. If you continue to lollygag then you'll surely get stuck in traffic. In fact, if you really want to get out of the house quickly then you'll need to skip breakfast. The idea saddens you, but these are the sacrifices that modern man must make in desperate times.

■ What do you do? ■

Turn to page 26 if you decide to skip breakfast to ensure a fast departure.

Turn to page 30 if you decide that a bowl of cereal would more than suffice and only require an extra few minutes.

If there is one thing the military has taught you, it's when to withhold classified information. Ann never understood the appeal of Scott Bakula nor his roles in Quantum Leap or as the fine starship commander in Star Trek Enterprise (and as a pilot, you have always been naturally interested in the lives of fellow aviators, whether real or imagined). It would be a waste of breath and would inevitably result in Ann bringing up something that she wanted to talk about… like the great taste of the Almond milk that she was recently pressuring you to try.

You reach over for the bottle of body-wash and immediately realize that it's nearly empty. You call out through the open door, "Ann?"

"Yes," she calls back from the bedroom.

"We need more body-wash."

"Really? Isn't that just for the shower."

"No, you can use it in the bath."

"Really?"

"Yeah, it lathers up well."

"Okay then. What type?" she asks, peeking in, her white dressing gown hanging partially open but revealing nothing interesting. A pimple and a stretch mark.

"It doesn't matter. Just nothing flowery or feminine."

"Maybe strawberry or peach?"

"No way. I can't be smelling like strawberries or peaches. Go with apple."

"Whatever," she says dismissively, "I'll see what's on sale."

"Only if its apple scented."

"Yes, yes, yes. Manly apple," she groans and leaves the room, once again granting you the solitude of a warm bath. You're in no rush to leave. You've worked hard your entire life and feel that a few extra soothing submerged minutes are warranted.

■ What do you do? ■

Turn to page 60 if you run more hot water.

Turn to page 62 if you turn on the bubble jets.

You pick up Ann's toothbrush and inspect the firm and strong bristles, wondering how she keeps them in such pristine shape. Did she not brush her teeth as frequently as you? Comparing her brimming pink toothbrush and your own limp and flayed green one, one would think that hers is brand new.

Just before squeezing a small line of aqua-blue paste, you wonder if this *is* perhaps a brand new brush. Did she buy one for herself but not for you? Every time you plucked a new toothbrush from the aisle at the supermarket you grabbed a second one for her, even if she didn't ask. It was an unspoken rule and you always assumed that she lived by this same code. For a man who'd spent half his life in the military, code and honor are things of paramount importance to you and the idea that your wife could potentially be living in accordance to a less disciplined moral system is, quite frankly, distressing. If she doesn't think about you when she's selecting toothbrushes from the supermarket aisle, would she think about you when approached by a young suitor at a bar?

Perhaps this is too great a leap to make—from selfish toothbrush consumption to infidelity—but a line has to be drawn somewhere. You're ready to trudge back to the bedroom and confront her right here, right now.

Where is *your* new toothbrush?

But then you notice a brand new blue toothbrush in the exact same style as Ann's, still in the plastic packaging, at the back of the bathroom counter. "Oh," you mutter, pleased that Ann did think about you. You pop the pristine head through the perforated cardboard and inspect the virginal bristles, excited by the prospect of all the plaque and bacteria that this was going to eradicate. You may be done with the war in Iraq, but the war against gingivitis never ends.

Just as you expected, your entire mouth feels refreshed and invigorated upon completion. Running your tongue over your teeth, you wish this fresh-from-the-dentist feeling could last. And then you look down and notice the stout container of floss on the counter. Flossing in the morning? This was always an evening activity. In fact, you're not sure if you've *ever* flossed first thing in the morning. Was there a reason? Or are you on the verge of discovering a new morning ritual?

■ What do you do? ■

Turn to page 31 if you decide to floss your teeth.

Turn to page 32 if you decide to go downstairs and get some coffee.

No, even in something as close-knit as a marriage there needs to be some degree of separation. If you begin to use Ann's toothbrush today, then what will come next tomorrow? Applying her deodorant? Borrowing her socks? Wearing her underwear? You are a man of distinction and honor, and dressing yourself in feminine undergarments is something that would prove disastrous to your career if word were ever to get out. Now, just how *word* would get out is beyond you—but you aren't prepared to risk it, either. In this age of Facebook and Youtube, nothing seems to be private any longer. You put down Ann's toothbrush and retrieve your own. You will not go down that dark path.

A few minutes later you twist on the water to the shower and give it a moment to warm up before testing the temperature with your right hand. It's still a little cool and so you wait a little longer.

It's while sitting on the closed toilet that you notice something on the wall across from you. Just beneath the medicine cabinet there is a long and thin horizontal streak of white running through the paint. Thinking this to be a scratch, you lean in close and run your fingernail over the mark. But it's not a scratch. It was never painted properly in the first place. How could you have never noticed this before? You and Ann repainted the house last month and somehow this glaring error had gone unseen for all these last weeks.

Well, you know who is to blame: Ann is the one who painted the ensuite. You were always suspect of her skills—you tried to convince her to take it easy, to go out and do something with Emma, but she refused. She insisted on 'helping' out. Some help she proved to be, you think, right as you hear her getting out of bed. You look towards the inviting shower and then towards the open bathroom door.

■ What do you do? ■

Turn to page 63 if you ask Ann whether or not she noticed this streak before.

Turn to page 65 if you leave it for now and just take that shower.

You give him a subtle nod—the non-committal greeting of all red-blooded men—and Roger does the same in reply. You then wonder just why he's mowing his lawn before eight in the morning, figuring that this could be a strange cultural quirk of being Chinese. Or perhaps it has to do with cutting the grass before the heat of the day? Although you're not sure about this, one thing is certain: Roger Wang can proudly lay claim to the best lawn on the block, perpetually as green as a can of 7-UP. If early morning mowing works for him, perhaps it would work for you, as well? In fact, it sounds like a perfect way to start a weekend: getting outside when the streets are still quiet and while the air is still crisp.

It's decided then; you're going to take Roger Wang's lead. This weekend, you're mowing the lawn while the rest of the world sleeps.

Upon turning on the radio, you're greeted by the rollicking sounds of Nickleback—always a surefire way to get the day started on a positive note. The traffic is light as you cruise through the winding roads of your neighborhood, tapping the steering wheel to the beat. Soon you merge onto the freeway and the roads are as clear and wide-open as a runway.

But then you're confronted with something horrible. The radio traffic reporter warns of an accident just a few miles up ahead. Already cars are backing up and commuters are urged to take an alternate route. You curse, knowing that the only other way to the airport would add at least fifteen minutes—and that's if everyone else doesn't have the same idea. Is the accident really going to slow things down that much? After all, there are four lanes in either direction.

Oh, how you wish that you could just pull back on your steering wheel and soar over all the other cars...

■ **What do you do?** ■

Turn to page 28 if you decide to stay on the freeway.

Turn to page 29 if you take the next exit and find another route to the airport.

You go with the thumbs up—a strange choice you realize, but only after it's too late—and Roger stares back with a cocked head. You then wonder if the Chinese even understand the meaning of a thumbs-up. Might it symbolize something different in his culture? Or could he confuse it with an outstretched middle finger? If so, that would explain his expression. You decide that you will educate Roger Wang on the pleasantries of a passing thumbs-up the next time you see him. It is part of your duty as a proud American to help assimilate newcomers.

Upon turning on the radio, you're greeted by the rollicking sounds of Nickleback—always a surefire way to get the day started on a positive note. The traffic is light as you cruise through the winding roads of your neighborhood, tapping the steering wheel to the beat. Soon you merge onto the freeway and the roads are as clear and wide-open as a runway.

But then you're confronted with something horrible. The radio traffic reporter warns of an accident just a few miles up ahead. Already traffic is backing up and commuters are urged to take an alternate route. You curse, knowing that the only other way to the airport would add at least another fifteen minutes—and that's if everyone else doesn't have the same idea. Is the accident really going to slow things down that much? After all, there are four lanes in either direction.

Oh, how you wish that you could just pull back on your steering wheel and fly over all the other cars...

■ What do you do? ■

Turn to page 28 if you decide to stay on the freeway.

Turn to page 29 if you take the next exit and find another way to the airport.

Really, what difference would a bowl of cornflakes make for your day, for your life? Sure, it would taste great. In fact, your mouth begins to water just from the thought of those mushy flakes soaking up the full-bodied 2% milk. But if there was one thing that you learned from basic training, it was that one's body requires a little tough-love from time-to-time. If you always succumb to a bowl of cornflakes in the morning, then next you'd start putting mayo on your sandwiches, or ordering gravy with your fries, or requesting blue cheese dressing with your Buffalo wings, or slathering icing on your cinnamon rolls… and when would it end? Morbidly obese, riding an electric scooter and eating all your meals from all-you-can-eat buffets?

No, you would not have the cornflakes this morning.

If you utilize these next minutes at home efficiently, you can still be on the road by 7:30. You would thus miss the worst of the traffic and get to the airport before 8:00. Just imagine the parking spot you could get!

Five minutes later, you descend the stairs into the kitchen, fully dressed. Ann is noticeably surprised as she offers you a cup of coffee.

"No thanks," you say. "I'm getting going right away."

"Why the rush?"

"I'm going to make good time if I leave now."

"But won't you just get in early?"

You chuckle. You can tell she was never in the military. "Oh, Honey…" You lean in and give her a kiss. "I'll see you this evening."

Seconds later, you're in the garage, swiping the keys to the Volvo off the hook as the door slowly lifts to reveal the beautiful sunny morning. Backing out, your neighbor Roger Wang is setting up his lawnmower and you give him a quick wave, impressed that he is taking care of his yard work so early in the day. That's why the Chinese are getting ahead, you think to yourself while driving along the winding suburban roads and out onto the freeway.

The traffic is light and you're able to cruise 7 mph over the speed limit. Aside from some speed-demon in a convertible Jaguar who changes lanes without even signaling, everyone is courteous and polite. Before you know it, you're taking the exit towards the airport and the staff parking lot. You look at the time on your dashboard and expel a grateful gasp.

7:52.

You can't believe it, unsure if you've ever had such a smooth and efficient commute before. Holding up your identification badge to the parking attendant, you proclaim: "I made it here in just over twenty minutes!"

"Wow," she begins. Or at least you thought it was just a beginning. But she says nothing more, waiting for you to drive on through.

Okay. She's lacking context. "Normally it takes more like thirty."

"Wow," she repeats in a lazy attempt at feigning enthusiasm.

"Yeah. It's going to be a good day."

"Sure will. You can go through now."

How could she ever understand? She spends her day inside a booth smaller than an airplane's restroom. Her world is confined and simple. Really, you can't blame her. But your life, on the other hand, is as wide open as the clear blue skies above. You know that today is going to be a good day. If you can cut away eight minutes from a thirty-minute drive, what's stopping you from shaving twice that much from an hour-long flight? People never expect an early flight.

Well, today, you're going to prove them wrong.

The End

■　■　■

It is a mistake staying on the freeway. All four eastbound lanes have come to a halt like a malfunctioning baggage carrousel—and there's nothing you can do about it.

What would normally take five minutes ends up taking thirty. When you approach the cause of the commotion—a flipped convertible Jaguar nearly sliced in half by a flatbed truck—you expel a mighty sigh of relief as the traffic thins out and you finally speed up. Creed's *With Arms Wide Open* comes onto the radio and you turn it up, figuring that this is a good omen. Tapping your hands on the steering wheel, those dire thoughts whilst stuck in traffic seem to vanish like the effervescence atop a freshly poured glass of 7-UP. Things are looking up. The worst is behind you, literally and figuratively.

As you approach the staff parking lot at the airport, you crane your neck back as a 737 roars overhead with its landing gear down, wobbling slightly to the left, to the right, and then onto the runway, expelling a puff of smoke a second before its screech. Flashing your ID to the gatekeeper, the attendant raises the bar and you're in. And in a way, you're home.

The End

■   ■   ■

Of all the fair journalists in this world, you have the utmost respect for the reports of traffic—they are your airborne kin hovering high above the masses, guiding the land-bearing folk through congestion and road-construction. Yes, if they advise you to take a detour, then you should take the detour. And good thing, too. Climbing up the off-ramp, you soon see the snaking traffic up ahead, all four lanes suddenly as clogged and busy as an airport security line the day before Thanksgiving. Yes, this was the right choice.

Away from the vast concrete freeway, you pass all sorts of colorful strip malls, car dealerships, Chinese and Mexican family restaurants, fast-food chains, big-box department stores and supermarkets. You then realize that you neglected to pack yourself a lunch and wonder if you should quickly turn into the approaching grocery store to purchase a packaged sandwich—it's either that or procuring a bag of pretzels and almonds on the plane. You don't really want to add any more time to your journey, but you also really don't want to have to subside on packaged snacks.

■ What do you do? ■

Turn to page 24 to stop into the supermarket to purchase a sandwich.

Turn to page 57 to carry on to the airport, accepting your inevitable snack-sized lunch.

Breakfast is the most important meal of the day. Sure, a bowl of cereal would hardly constitute a complete and nourishing meal, but it is better than nothing. And to be honest, consuming a bowl of cornflakes was one of your guilty pleasures—right up there with enjoying a cold glass of 7-UP after work. There is something about a soggy reconstituted chip of cornmeal that delights your taste buds. In fact, the more soggy, the better. You never enjoyed any of those 'crunchy' cereals, the ones with nuts and coatings that made them somewhat impervious to moisture. Who wants to chomp down and risk losing a filling first thing in the morning?

You begin to salivate upon visualizing a heaping bowl of cornflakes soaking in a pool of smooth 2% milk. You quickly get dressed and dash down the stairs, wasting no time in retrieving a deep ceramic bowl from the cupboard and placing it on the granite countertop. Flipping open the cardboard top to the cereal box, you delicately lift the bottom and shake out its contents, admiring the golden flakes as they tumble down into the bowl. Finally, you open the fridge and grab the milk, pointing out its waxy spout.

But then you read the container:

Buttermilk.

You expel a long sigh, your heart racing. That was close. Slowly, you lower the milk and leave it on the counter, looking back in the fridge for the normal milk. But there is none. It then comes to you: Ann used up the last of the 2% milk when making a smoothie yesterday evening. You shake your head, dejected from coming so close to having a bowl of cornflakes. But there's nothing you can do about it.

Or is there?

■ What do you do? ■

Turn to page 67 if you decide to use the buttermilk in your cornflakes.

Turn to page 68 if you pour the cereal back into the box and get on with your day.

You firmly believe that variety is the spice of life and decide to attempt the unexpected. You're going to floss first thing in the morning. With a sly smile on your face, you unravel a few feet of floss and break it off before wrapping a couple of inches around your right index finger. Looking into the mirror, you lean forward with your mouth wide open and maneuver the waxy string to the bottom right molar. Or, actually that would be your bottom *left* molar, considering that you're looking into your reflection.

No, it's the bottom right, you realize after a little more reflection (no pun intended).

Sliding the floss in behind the tooth, you tug back and forth a couple times and move on to the next tooth. This one is trickier—that old crown always seemed to be a little oversized and makes tough work of getting the floss down beneath the gum line. You remember your dentist advising you to get some special floss for the crown but you never believed him, assuming it was all part of some kickback scheme that all dentists are privy to. There are just some things in life not worth wasting money on.

By the time you reach the other side of your mouth you pause to evaluate this experience, now halfway through. You have to be honest: it wasn't what you hoped for. Your teeth don't feel any cleaner. In fact, your gums are now just a little raw. That's it. There is no need to carry on any further and you toss the used floss into the garbage.

There is a reason people don't floss in the morning: it's a waste of precious time.

Turn to page 32.

No, it is time to get on with the morning. Stepping out from the bathroom, you're immediately drawn to the aroma of freshly brewed coffee wafting from the kitchen. You can't wait for a good *cuppajoe* (as you like to refer to it in your more jovial moods) but then you stop and once again run your tongue over your freshly cleaned teeth. Would it not be a better idea to get into the routine of drinking coffee *before* brushing your teeth? The way you're doing it now seems completely backwards, like showering before going to the gym or seeking international approval in advance of conducting an overseas invasion. Really, what is stopping you from taking the entire brewing operation—coffee maker, grounds, filters, spoons—up to your ensuite? You could even utilize the never-used timer feature as a sort of aromatic alarm clock. Honestly, what better way would there be to wake up than to the gentle percolating pops, whispering hisses, and drifting scent of brewing coffee? You hurry down the steps to tell Ann about this great new idea.

"Good morning," you say, almost short of breath. "I have an idea: tell me what you think."

"Okay," Ann says, still in her nightgown, rinsing off a spoon in the sink.

"Why don't we move the coffee maker into the bathroom upstairs? We can set it up every night before going to sleep and use the timer to wake us up in the morning. That way when we get out of bed we can pour ourselves a cup of coffee while still in the bathroom."

Ann turns off the tap and slowly twists her neck to look at you with her piercing brown eyes. She simply stares for several prolonged seconds before shaking her head. "Using sink water from the bathroom? That's gross."

"What do you mean? It's water. Water is water."

"No. It's bathroom water. It's not the same. It's not filtered."

She has a point. The water from the kitchen sink runs through a purification system—although you remain skeptical as to what it actually does besides reduce the water pressure and demand monthly filters. In your more cynical moods, you figure it's just another scam, like fancy dental floss, chiropractors, or the United Nations.

"Anyhow," she withdraws a mug from the cupboard and carries it over to the coffee maker. "I made some coffee the old fashioned way this morning, if that's all right with you. Do you want a cup?"

You lazily nod a few times (wondering how practical it would be to install a water filter onto your ensuite bathroom sink) before remembering what happened the last time Ann made the coffee. It was a disaster. She carelessly used the grounds left over from when her sister Sarah stayed over last month, brewing some of the cheapest coffee around—one of those brands that is packaged exclusively in gallon tins plastered with the words *PREMIUM QUALITY*. Never a good sign.

■ **What do you do?** ■

Turn to page 58 if you accept the offer as usual.

Turn to page 59 if you ask for the coffee in a travel mug in case you need to dump it.

You suddenly and deftly veer out from your lane as if to out-maneuver an enemy MiG 29, pulling into the vast and nearly vacant grocery store parking lot. There are literally hundreds of empty parking stalls for you to choose from and the plethora of easy options brings a smile to your face usually reserved for weather reports of strong tailwinds. If only everything in life could be as easy as finding supermarket parking before eight in the morning on a weekday, you think.

As you stroll through the quiet aisles, you wonder why you don't do this more often: early morning weekday shopping. You even figure it would be worth waking up thirty minutes earlier just to take advantage of the empty aisles, open tills and countless shopping carts. The aroma of freshly baked bread fills the air as you approach the deli counter and its array of pre-made sandwiches. You look at the many choices and for a moment it seems like this will prove to be an arduous decision. Which one? Chicken salad? Roast beef? Ham and cheese? Turkey and cranberry? But then you see it: the tuna-salad special. There's no need to look any longer. You pluck the triangular plastic package and then saunter towards the cashiers, several open but not a single customer in line.

You almost don't want this to end.

"Good morning," the cashier says while putting her phone back into her pocket.

You read her nametag. "Good morning, Taryl." You leave the sandwich on the black plastic conveyor and smile. "It's sure quiet this morning."

"Oh, yeah. It's nice, isn't it? It'll be crazy a little later on, though."

"Do you like it better when it's busy or when it's quiet?"

"Oh, I don't know. A little bit of both, you know?"

"Yeah."

"If it's too quiet, time crawls. But if it's too busy, it's just too stressful."

"I can imagine."

"Is this all?" she says in reference to the sandwich and you're not sure what she's implying. Does she think you're going to ask for a pack of cigarettes? A bus-pass? What kind of person does she think you are?

You decide to find out: "What do you mean?"

"Like, you know, do you want some gum or maybe a drink?"

Ah, the classic up-sell, you think while gently shaking your head ... but then pause. "Actually, a cold can of 7-UP does sound refreshing."

"We don't sell cans, but we have bottles in the fridge just behind you."

"A bottle of 7-UP?" Your eyes open wide like a passenger offered a free upgrade to a business-class seat. "You have glass bottles of 7-UP? I haven't had one of those since I was a kid."

"Oh, no. Plastic bottles."

You sigh with obvious disappointment. "Oh. No thanks, then."

"You sure?"

"I only like my soda from a can—although I would have taken up the opportunity to relive some childhood memories by enjoying a tall, curvy glass bottle of 7-UP. I wonder why they stopped making them?"

"Probably a safety thing. You know, kids dropping bottles and stuff?"

"Huh. I can't think that it would have really been that big of a deal. Those bottles were surprisingly durable."

Taryl then shrugs her shoulders. "I wouldn't know. I only remember cans and plastic bottles."

"Really? You didn't have glass bottles for soda when you were a kid?"

"Nope. I guess I'm too young."

You wonder if this Taryl lady can really be *that* much younger than you. You can't see her being any less than twenty years old—but then you realize what that entails. She's half your age. When she was still in diapers, you were in Iraq. She's probably never even heard of Saddam Hussein, or Chumbawamba for that matter. You truly are getting old.

"So," she then asks, "are you going to get a Sprite?"

Your reply is curt: "I said 7-UP."

"Oh, sorry. Do you want one?"

"No, I guess not. It wouldn't stay cold. Besides, I can get one on the plane."

"So, this is it, then?" she asks again.

"I think it is."

"Okay." She slides the sandwich through the scanner and it beeps—once. You always make sure that it only beeps once. Taryl then asks, looking at your lunch, "Hey, so how are these, anyhow?"

"I don't know. I don't think I've tried this exact one before. But I do like a tuna salad sandwich."

"Tuna? That's a different choice."

"Is it?"

"Yeah. I don't know. Doesn't seem to be the usual, you know?"

You wince and slowly nod before shaking your head. You don't know. There were at least a half-dozen tuna-salad sandwiches to choose from. How unique could your decision really be? "I guess."

She holds it up to inspect it closer. "The bread looks good. You like bread with seeds and stuff in it?"

"I do. A little crunch is nice."

"Plus those flax seeds are supposed to be really good for you, aren't they?"

"High in Omega-3 oils, yes."

"I think that's what makes a sandwich for me," Taryl says, nodding.

You're not sure what she's referring to. "Omega 3 oils?"

"No," Taryl laughs, "Tasty bread."

"Ah," you nod in wholehearted agreement. "You're right."

"I should really try these. I usually buy my lunch at like Subway or something."

"I hope it's good. I do love a tuna sandwich."

"I've always been a fan of chicken salad."

"That is a good one too."

"Huh, you'll have to tell me how it is."

"Sure," you say, then wonder just how you'd ever relay to her your evaluation before noticing her placing the sandwich in an otherwise empty plastic bag. "Actually, you don't need to put it in a bag."

"Oh, do you have one of those reusable bags with you?"

"No, I'll just carry it with me."

"Yeah, no need to put more into the landfills, right?"

"Exactly."

"Okay then. That's easy for me." She passes over the sandwich.

"Thanks."

"So, will that be cash or credit?"

That is a good question. Normally you'd pay in cash, but all you have is a hundred dollar bill and figure that such a lofty denomination would only create hassle. Plus all the change would get cumbersome. You make your decision. You pull out your wallet, "You know, I think I'll pay with credit."

"Sounds good." She taps the screen in front of her and then adds, "You can swipe it through when you're ready."

"Sure," you reply with your wallet on the narrow counter as you flip through the many cards within. Normally, you always leave your MasterCard Titanium adjacent to the bills in order to aid in its expedient retrieval. But it's not in its spot and you're forced to finger through all the many customer patronage cards, old gift-cards, various business cards, your library card, your video rental card, your driver's license, some old folded receipts, the supermarket club card—"Wait, don't you want this?" you hold the patronage card up in the air.

"Oh, yeah. Sorry. I really should have asked." Taryl takes it from you and swipes it through. "There you go."

"Thanks," you put the card back in and resume your search.

"Oh, it looks like you don't have any savings today," she adds with a lazy frown.

"That's okay."

"But you earned five points."

"That's five more points than I had yesterday."

"Every little bit helps."

"Of course." You get to the end of your cards and sigh, unsure about where your credit card is. "Huh," you mutter and wonder if you should try looking through it again or just pay in cash.

"Can't find your credit card?"

"No. I'm sure it should be in here."

"Take your time. No one's in line."

As tempting as it would be to just pay in cash, you know you have to get to the bottom of this mystery. Returning to the start, right by that one hundred dollar bill, you once again flip through the cards, methodically and carefully. "Well look at this!" you then exclaim.

"What is it?" Taryl asks.

"It's a video store coupon. A two-for-one rental. I was looking for this last year before the local Blockbuster closed down."

"That would have been useful."

This gets you thinking and you pause again to ask: "Do you still see a lot of coupons on a day to day basis?"

"Of course."

"I wasn't sure if they are still common. I can't think of the last time I used a coupon at a supermarket."

"Haven't you ever seen *Extreme Couponing* on TV? I think it's bigger than ever."

"*Extreme Couponing*? What's that?"

Taryl seems shocked to hear of your ignorance. "Really? You've never heard of *Extreme Couponing*?"

You would think that it was a seminal television series from her reaction. "No."

"Oh, it's crazy."

"What's it about?"

"People buying lots with coupons."

"That's it?"

"They get some pretty crazy deals. This one lady bought like a hundred boxes of Hot Pockets for nothing."

"Nothing at all?"

"Nothing at all." Taryl repeats for emphasis.

You have always enjoyed a steamy and gooey Hot Pocket, although Ann is adamant that something so nutritionally vacant has no place in your home. But would she turn down a deep-freeze full of *free* Hot Pockets? You think not. While initially revolted by the idea of watching a television show about people using coupons, it does have a strange appeal. "You know, that actually does sound rather interesting. I do enjoy a bargain as much as the next."

"Especially in these tough economic times," Taryl adds.

"Very true." You look at the Blockbuster coupon in your hand and sigh. "I guess they'll be no video rental episodes of *Extreme Couponing*, however. If only I would have used it sooner."

"Maybe another location will honor it. We do that here with competitor's coupons."

"I'm not sure there are any video rental stores left. I think the Internet has wiped out that industry."

Taryl nods. "They were old fashioned."

You try to repress a frown. Old fashioned? You remember when videocassettes came out and the video store was one of the most exciting places around. These wondrous stores granted people the ability to bring the cinema home; before, the only option was to wait years for an edited version to be broadcast on television.

"But you know," Taryl adds, "Kinda cool in a way."

"They were," you nod, "but you are right. The future is here and now, speaking of which, I should keep hunting for my card. Can you get rid of this?" You hold out the now invalid coupon.

"Sure."

"Will it be recycled?"

"No, I only have a trash can."

"Hmm, then I think I will keep it in my pocket. I try to recycle as much as I can, you know, do my part for Mother Earth and all that."

"Me too!" she exclaimed, "I wish we did it here, I don't know why we don't. I will suggest that to the manager. You have no idea how many extra receipts are left here." Taryl then pauses and cocks her head to the side. "Aren't you a pilot, though?"

You nod in agreement, knowing how women love a pilot.

"Well," Taryl says, "I heard that planes are terrible for the environment. That they pollute the same as like a billion cars."

"A billion cars?" You laugh, "That can't be right."

"Okay then, I don't know. A million?"

"I'm sure that's not right."

"Well, I saw something about that on the news."

"I don't know. I just fly the planes."

"Sorry, I didn't mean to sound rude there."

"No, it's okay."

"It must be really cool being a pilot, flying all over the place and stuff."

"Yes, it has its perks. But I try to stay close to home. I don't want to be away from my daughter for long."

"Ah, you have a daughter? How old is she?"

"She's four."

"That's the best age, I think. I love kids."

"Do you have any?"

"Kids? No." Taryl nearly scoffs and you wonder just how she can really love children considering her reaction. "So, what's her name?"

"Emma."

"My aunt's name is Emma."

"Really?"

"Yeah! What a coincidence."

You wonder if that really constitutes being 'a coincidence' but don't press her on the issue, instead sticking your hand down your pocket to pretend to look for something when really just scratching an itchy testicle.

You hope she doesn't notice and her facial expression gives nothing away. In relief, you scratch the other side, not for need but for a little pleasure. It feels satisfactory.

But then you shake your head and recall what you're supposed to be doing—finding that credit card. You finger through your wallet for just a few more seconds before attempting a different course of action: searching the various pockets in your trousers and blazer, although it doesn't take long to realize that it's not there. Did someone take it? Were you pick-pocketed? After a moment's deliberation, you accept the implausibility of such a situation; how could even the most experienced criminal steal one's credit card without also procuring the wallet? You put both hands on the counter and expel a long, disappointed sigh. "I don't know where it is."

"What's that?"

"My MasterCard Titanium."

"Oh yeah. When's the last time you used it?"

"I don't know. Maybe yesterday at lunch?"

"Did you buy your lunch from here?"

"No, at the airport."

"Oh. Do you think you should call your credit card company?"

You groan, knowing this is the thing to do but detesting the mere thought of the impending hassle. But then you remember. You both smile and groan. "Ah, that's it."

"What's that?"

"I used it last night to purchase something online. I must have left it on the desk by the computer."

Taryl laughs, "I do that all the time. What were you buying?"

"I was looking at crown molding. We painted just last month and now I'm thinking of how we can better frame the spaces."

She looks at you quizzically. "Crown molding? What's that?"

Initially you assume that she must be kidding—who doesn't know what crown molding is? But then you nod, realizing that this *is* just a simple cashier. "It's the decorative woodwork that runs along the perimeter of a room between the wall and the ceiling."

Taryl slowly nods. "Oh yeah."

Although she clearly doesn't know what you're talking about, you figure that there's no point in pressing the matter any further. You nod along as if waiting for her to say something else.

"So," she begins, "What are you going to do?"

"I'm not sure. I've been thinking about a beveled look, but my wife and I are still open to different ideas."

"No, about paying."

"Oh." Yes. The sandwich. You still haven't paid for it. "I guess I'll have to use cash." You withdraw the single, clean and crisp one hundred dollar bill and pass it over. "Here you go."

She grimaces as if being told of a lengthy flight delay. "Actually, I don't know if I have enough change for that. Hold on," she takes the bill and walks over to the customer service counter, speaking out of earshot with another lady. It's amazing how often the attempted use of a one hundred dollar bill seems to become such an ordeal for retail businesses. Why even print $100 bills if every cashier seems to think that they are somehow unwieldy? You're not coming in with a burlap sack of silver coins, after all.

Taryl returns from customer service with her supervisor, a middle-aged woman seemingly without a single noteworthy feature. She's just a middle-aged woman. But then you read that her name is Misty—an odd name for a supermarket supervisor. You would find it very difficult taking orders from someone with such a name. A stripper, yes. A manager, no. And if your parents named you Misty, then you would have undoubtedly changed it as soon as possible. Of course, if your name was Misty then that would also imply that you were a woman... and then everything would be different. You surely wouldn't have become an elite fighter pilot; that industry remains the domain of men.

"Hello," Misty says with some rolls of coins and packages of cash in her hand. "You don't have anything smaller?"

"No, unfortunately not. I was going to pay with my credit card but I left it on the desk counter back at home."

"Yeah, I heard." Misty says. "Taryl told me the whole crazy story."

"Oh," you reply, wondering if it was really necessary for Taryl to inform her supervisor of all these things.

"It's not a problem," she continues, "It'll just take a moment. I need to make some change for her."

"Of course."

She takes your crisp $100 bill and tucks it under the black plastic tray before filling up the partitions with fives, tens, twenties and a new roll of quarters which doesn't break the first time she clubs it against the corner of the counter. She tries again and this time the beige paper wrapping rips apart to reveal the shiny new quarters. She dumps the coins onto the tray and shuts the drawer. Afterwards she signs some sort of log on a clipboard. "Okay, all good."

"Great," you reply.

Misty then looks at your tuna-fish sandwich. "Mmm. That looks good."

"Yeah, I hope so."

"I like a good tuna sandwich."

"Me too."

"Our deli department makes some fantastic sandwiches."

"I haven't had this one before."

"Then I think you'll love it."

You're not sure what else to say. You've been though all this before. "Yup."

"But, you know who makes the best sandwiches?" Misty says, pointing her finger, "That place... what's it called?"

"Where is it?"

"It's just down the street from here. There's a few of them around," she says, the name of it on the tip of her tongue.

"I hate it when that happens," you say. "When you can't remember the name of a place."

"Oh, it happens to me all the time."

"That's called Dysnomia," you say.

"Really? There's a word for that?"

"Yeah. If it happens a lot."

"That's funny. There's a big word for when you can't remember a word!"

You're not sure how it is funny. In fact, you know that Dysnomia can be a debilitating condition and you'd recommend Misty get diagnosed if not for her potentially finding it insulting.

Misty then looks to Taryl, "Do you know the name of that sandwich place, just down the street?"

Taryl slowly shakes her head. "I don't know. What's it look like?"

"It's small, has yellow walls. You get to pick your own vegetables."

"I don't know," Taryl repeats with a grimace. "Subway?"

Misty claps her hands, "That's it! Subway. They make the best sandwiches, I think."

"Me too!" Taryl says, "I usually go there for lunch."

You nod along in agreement, having to admit that Subway does make a consistently delicious product—although you'd rather her refer to them as *subs*. A sandwich is made with slices of bread. A sub is made on a long but narrow bun. Calling a sub a sandwich is like calling a flatbread a pizza or ordering a 7-UP only to be delivered a glass of Sprite. There is a difference and people should use the correct terminology.

But all these thoughts then make you wonder if it was a mistake buying this tuna-salad sandwich from the supermarket—couldn't you have gotten a freshly made submarine sandwich for approximately the same price?

Apparently your expression is an open book as Misty then asks, "Are you okay? Is there anything we can do for you?"

"Actually, all this talk about getting a sub from Subway is making me wonder if I should have just picked up one from there. There's one in the airport I could easily stop off on my way."

"But you know, there's a problem with that," Taryl says, having clearly thought about this before.

"What's that?" you ask.

"If you're not going to eat it until lunch, then it would get really soggy. Subs are only good if you can eat it right away."

She has just made an excellent point and you nod, impressed with the reasoning of someone who didn't know what crown molding was. "Oh, you're right. All that lettuce would make it soggy."

"And don't forget about the tomatoes." Misty adds. "They have a lot of water in them."

"Actually, I don't put tomatoes on."

"Really?" Misty seems very surprised—too surprised just to learn of someone not consuming tomatoes on a sandwich. "You don't like tomatoes? I love tomatoes."

"Oh, no, I like tomatoes, just not on a sandwich."

Taryl nods along, "My brother is the same way. His favorite meal growing up was spaghetti and meatballs, but he would get furious if Mom would put tomatoes in the salad."

"Couldn't he just pick them out?" Misty thankfully asks since you were thinking the exact same question. This brother of Taryl's is sure sounding like a bit of a prince.

"Yeah, but you know what kids can be like. Just picky."

"Hmm," you merely add, thinking about your daughter Emma and hoping that she will not grow up to be so particular. You make another mental note: this time to ensure there are some fresh tomatoes in tonight's salad. Dietary habits start at a young age and you would have to make sure not to coddle her.

"Okay, then. Enjoy your sandwich." Misty taps the counter a couple of times before returning to customer service where she promptly resumes reading the magazine that she was flipping through before.

Taryl limply smiles towards you as if you two had met in an elevator. Nothing is exchanged and she seems uncertain about what to do or why you're still standing there. And then she remembers. "Oh yeah, the change." She counts through the restocked piles of bills, "You don't mind if I give you ten dollars of your change in quarters, do you?"

You nod, not really listening, wondering if maybe you should run over to the produce section while you're here and pick up a tomato just to test on Emma later on in the evening. "Sure." But then you clue in—ten dollars in quarters? Good Gosh. "Sorry, that's far too much change. I thought you just got your register restocked?"

"I know, but that's mostly for later today. If I run short there can be real problems." She smiles and starts counting out the many, many quarters.

"What?"

"Okay, I can give you four twenties and a ten max, or five tens and eight fives, but the rest needs to be in small change."

"Really? I'm sorry, but I still have to clear the security at the airport, which means I have to empty out my pockets. All that change takes forever to unload from the basket. And I'm always worried I will forget some... not that I'm cheap, but you know, money is money."

Taryl nods, "I never thought about that. Okay, let me think about this."

You let her think about that. She stands motionless before her open cash register, arms folded, staring at the bills and coins as if waiting for something to happen. You can't help but think how much easier this all would have been if you had just made more of a point of putting your

MasterCard back into your wallet. You remember when you were a kid how your mother would sew your mittens together with a long string. Perhaps a similar idea for credit cards could prove prudent? Maybe something like fishing line or an elastic material that could allow one to withdraw it with ease but also snap back into place when finished? But that would never work. All the different cards would surely become tangled into a horrendous knot. No, it seems that in life there are just some problems that can't be solved.

Returning to the situation at hand, the cashier still hasn't moved and you finally ask: "So…"

She then continues: "Okay, what about nine tens? I'd be pushing it, but I think I can do that."

"Let me think a minute." Nine tens? An interesting proposition, you have to admit. Having nine tens could be handy plus you can't remember the last time you had so many ten dollar bills—probably not since you were twelve and mowing people's lawns on a long weekend blitz. For the sake of reminiscing, you decide to agree. "Okay. Nine tens will do." You're actually excited by the prospect.

She looks in the till and then frowns. "Actually, I can't really do that. How about eight tens and two fives and ones plus change."

"Okay, okay," you agree, realizing it's time to go. In fact, you wonder just how much time you've spent at the checkout as it is.

She looks back in the till, not saying a word.

"Is everything all right?" you ask.

"Honestly, I don't really feel all that comfortable, you know? I need more change so let me just call my supervisor and get more."

"Sure," you reluctantly agree, not really having a choice.

You expect Taryl to walk back over to the customer service deck, but instead she merely picks up the phone beside her, "Supervisor to check out eight." Her voice echoes out from the intercom and through the store.

A moment later Misty returns, "Is there a problem?"

"I need more change."

"But I just gave you some."

"I know, but I don't think that it will be enough. It could be busy later. I want to be prepared…"

It's while Taryl explains her situation that you realize that Misty's blouse has opened partly, her nametag now directing wandering eyes down

45

to her cleavage where you notice the sliver of a blue tattoo on her right breast. Is it a scorpion? A pitchfork? Too hard to tell. Either way, the work looks cheap and not appealing on a middle-aged woman's bosom. She could use some laser surgery to remedy the matter; those lasers seem to be able to do anything these days. Laser guided missiles. Laser eye surgery. Laser hair removal. Laser pointers...

"Oh no!" Taryl suddenly exclaims the moment Misty leaves.

"What?"

"The drawer is jammed now. This always happens on till eight."

"But it was just closed?"

"I know, I know." She starts shoving the drawer and it slides in another few inches before refusing to budge any further.

"So, what can we do?"

"I guess I could run it through over there on till nine."

"Can't you get your supervisor to do something?"

"No, we'll need to get one of the techs in to fix this. Although I will need a supervisor to verify how much money is visible." She groans, "I hate it when this happens."

"That's okay," you follow her over to the adjacent till, sandwich in hand, and place it down on the counter, watching as she sets up the new register.

"This should just take a moment."

"Of course."

As she logs in, you can't help but notice her employee code: 58008. It's hard to repress a smile as you recall all those times in elementary math class that you'd type that exact same number into your calculator before flipping it over to revel in the display: BOOBS. For years this was the first thing you'd do upon withdrawing your calculator from your desk, or anytime you borrowed someone else's, for that matter. You'd tap Jeff Smith on the shoulder and show him the display. Oh yeah. You'd both snicker and nod, careful not to attract undue attention of the teacher or any surrounding girls. Sure, you also learned of 53118008, yet that seemed almost a little too forced, too convoluted.

But your reminiscent grin soon droops as you wonder about kids nowadays; do they have any appreciation for such simple numerical thrills now that everyone seems to have access to a smart phone? Probably not. They can look at actual boobs. How can five block digits ever compare?

You sigh with melancholy acceptance: the past can never be found again.

Taryl hands the sandwich back to you. "Are you okay?"

"Oh, I'm fine. Just remembering the good old days… but actually…" you notice something and hold the package closer to your eyes.

"Is something wrong?"

"I don't know. It looks like there's something in the package there."

"Oh, what is it?"

"I think it's a hair. A black hair." You say *you think*, but you are actually absolutely certain.

"Good golly, I'm so sorry. That's disgusting." She then runs her hand through her own long black hair. "You don't think it's one of mine?"

"Not unless you were the one who made the sandwich. The hair is inside the packaging."

"No, that's done by our deli department. Do you want me to get you a new one?"

"Actually," if you wanted a way out of this entire situation, then this is it. You could shake your head, assure her that you'll not bother with the sandwich, leave the supermarket and pick up something from Subway. After all, who said you'd *have* to put lettuce on the sub? This packaged sandwich didn't have any vegetables at all. But no. You've committed enough time here as it is and pulling out at this late stage in the game would be like if America had withdrawn from Iraq before the mission was accomplished. You have a duty to see this through. "No, that's all right. I can go do it."

"Oh, no." She shakes her head. "I'll get it."

"Is something wrong?" Misty then calls out from her customer service desk.

"Yeah, there's a hair in this man's sandwich."

"What?" Misty replies, seemingly angry.

"I know!" Taryl says, shaking her head in disbelief. "It's a disgrace."

"No," Misty shakes her head, "I didn't hear you. What did you say?"

Taryl holds up your sandwich, "There's a black hair in this sandwich."

"What?"

"Did you hear that?"

"Yeah, I heard. That's terrible. I'm so sorry. I'll go get him another one."

"No, no," you assure, "I can get it myself."

"No way, Jose. It's the least I can do." Misty then trundles away from her station towards the other side of the supermarket. You wish that she'd walk at least a little faster—you stroll at a faster pace than she supposedly hurries. And why did she use the expression, "*No way, Jose?*" Does anyone actually say that anymore? Apparently if your name is Misty, then yes.

Taryl smiles and looks away, first to the screen and then behind her to customer service. You rest an elbow on the counter and look across the store, Misty now out of sight, waiting for her to return. But she is nowhere in sight. Turning back to Taryl, you find this silence awkward and struggle to thinks of topics for small talk. But isn't it *her* job to think of things to say? Isn't that part of her training? It's definitely not your job. You're a pilot. You only speak to the common people to inform them of the most crucial facts: cruising altitude, estimated journey time, upcoming turbulence and destination weather.

You crane your neck back, wondering just where Misty could be. The supermarket isn't *that* big. What could she be doing? You pass a glance towards Taryl and she smiles, ready to say something. But then she looks down to her cell phone in her pocket.

"So, it sure is a nice morning," you say.

"Yeah," she puts the phone away and nods in agreement. "It's real warm."

"Especially for the morning."

"It's nice."

"It sure is." You look around again, but there's still no sign of the supervisor. "They say it's supposed to rain tomorrow."

"Really?" Taryl frowns. "That's too bad."

"I guess the nice weather can't last forever."

"Yeah. Not unless we lived in California, I guess."

"True. But it gets too hot there, unless you live right on the coast. I was stationed near San Diego for a while and the climate wasn't really for me."

"I wouldn't know. I've never been there."

"Really? Not even to Disneyland as a kid?"

"I went to Disneyland, but it was in Florida."

"That's Disneyworld," you say.

"Are you sure?"

You're actually insulted but stop yourself from scoffing. What would make a cashier doubt the geographical knowledge of a pilot? "Yes. I'm sure."

"Huh. Then what's the one in New York called?"

"I don't think there's a Disney-themed resort in New York."

"Really? Maybe I'm thinking of something else."

"You must be." Again, where the hell is Misty? There were several other tuna-salad sandwiches to choose from; she didn't need to order a new one made. You're tempted just to leave—but they have your $100 bill. Your departure would get messy. You didn't have an appropriate exit strategy.

"Huh." Taryl says while popping out a piece of gum from a foil bubble pack. "Do you want one?"

"Sorry?"

"Gum? You want some gum?"

"Uh, no thank you." You never cared for strangers casually offering gum. It didn't make sense. Would she offer you a few Smarties? A Skittle? Why was gum any different?

"So, why is that, then, you think?"

"What do you mean?"

"I mean, about Disneyland in New York."

"There is no Disneyland in New York."

"I know, I know. I mean, why isn't there one? You think a place like New York would be a big enough city for something like that."

The answer to her question seems obvious. "Well, I think the weather would be an issue. People wouldn't want to go on rides in the winter in New York."

"Yeah," she chews her gum especially loud, "but they could cover it. You know, like a big dome or something."

What can be said in reply to such a comment? You look back around and notice Misty returning at a pace appropriate for someone sauntering to the pool while on holiday. She then holds up a brand-new tuna-fish sandwich. "Here you go," she says somehow with both a smile and a sigh. "Sorry it took so long. I had to have them make you a new one."

That's strange, you think, as you know there were others—and for a moment wonder if this is even a new sandwich. How can you be sure that she didn't just open up the wrapping, take out the hair, and then tape it back together? You want to ask her. Something seems wrong about all of this. But what could you really say? "Thanks." That's all.

"Sorry for that." Misty repeats before handing over a voucher.

"What's this?"

"It's a coupon for 50% off your next sandwich purchase."

"Oh." 50% off on your *next* purchase? Shouldn't you be getting 50% off of this purchase? Or maybe not pay anything at all? Customer service in this country is really going to hell.

Misty then adds: "I think it must have been one of the Mexicans."

"What's that?"

"The hair. I think it must have come from one of the Mexicans in the deli department."

"Okay…"

Misty nods and sighs and then finally leaves, strolling back to her station. Taryl taps a few things on her screen and then asks, "What did we agree on again, with the whole change thing?"

"I think it was going to be eight tens and two fives and ones."

"Hmmm," Taryl nods with a strange reluctance. "Yeah, that was it. Okay." She then taps yet more points on the screen as if operating a cash register is akin to piloting a jet. How can there be so many buttons? You then turn around and notice a trashy gossip magazine, the type Ann is always leaving under the sink in the ensuite bathroom. On the glossy cover are three supposedly famous women in skimpy bathing suits, their cellulite highlighted with bright circles and arrows. What if the paparazzi took pictures of you while you were on holiday in Hawaii last spring? What would they have highlighted? Your hands immediately grab the flab around your belly and then go and clutch you own butt. In alarm, you realize it looks like you just scratched you ass. You slowly turn only to find Taryl staring at you, her eyes betraying the superficial smile on her face.

"So," you clear your throat, wondering if you should tell her that you *weren't* scratching yourself—although doing so would only imply guilt. "I guess that's it."

"Yeah," she slowly nods and finalizes the purchase with a final poke at the screen. The register pops open and the receipt prints. "Oh, crap," she then mutters.

"What's that?"

"The paper for the receipt is out. I have to change the roll."

"I don't need the receipt. I can just go."

"Sorry, but I can't give you the change until the receipt is printed. It's company policy."

"Okay." The register is still open. You can see all the appropriate bills and coins. But protocol is protocol—and as a man of the military, you do rather respect this.

"It will just be a second," she says while pulling out the coiled stub of pink-tinged paper that remains.

Another customer then saunters up from behind you, a bearded old man wearing a ratty wool coat; a curious wardrobe choice considering that the high today is due to push 80 degrees. You'd describe him as a hobo, although you're not really sure if people use the term 'hobo' anymore. It's definitely more palatable than 'bum' and more charming than the rather characterless 'homeless person,' which seems to be the norm. "Good morning, Taryl," he says, revealing a missing front tooth. "It's like the end of the world out there."

Taryl replies with a sigh. "Sure, Randy." She spools the new roll of paper in and closes the top of the printer. "Okay, there. That's it."

"Great," you say.

But then she groans. "Oh. Just wait. It's still not working." She opens the printer and pulls out the paper once again.

"What you got there?" Randy then asks, only after which you realize that he's talking to you.

"Me? Oh, just this sandwich."

"Looks good! What kind is it?"

"Uh, tuna."

"Tuna!" Randy nearly yells, suddenly appearing to be angry over your choice of lunch. "Why tuna?"

"Uhm, I'm not sure." You can't help but notice the strange mix of odors emanating from the man—predominantly bacon and mouthwash. You take a step away from him but he immediately takes an equivalent step closer. "I just like tuna."

"No, no, no. Don't get tuna. Ham. Get the ham."

"Okay." You really don't want to engage in a conversation with this clearly unstable vagrant and ask Taryl: "It is working yet?"

"Just about." Contrary to what she says, however, she seems no closer to resolving the issue. At least three feet of the brand new roll is now unwound and draped to the floor.

"If I had money, I'd get me a ham sandwich." Randy says and accentuates his point by slapping the black rubber conveyor. "That's the best."

"Okay, point taken."

"What you do? You police?"

"Uh, no. I'm a pilot."

"Holy Jesus juniper!" Randy exclaims with both a sneer and much spittle. "You fly planes?"

You're not sure if Randy's last sentence is a question or a statement and decide to only nod and smile before looking back to Taryl, hoping for an imminent resolution to her problem.

"I was a pilot once," Randy says.

"No you weren't." Taryl retorts while perhaps finalizing the paper.

"Oh yeah, maybe I wasn't."

"Okay!" she says, much to your relief. "It's working." She taps a button on her screen and the receipt rises from the printer like bubbles in a cool glass of 7-UP. "Sorry about that."

"It's not a problem," you say out of instinct, although it's completely dishonest. In this digital age, why is there still a need for paper receipts? Couldn't there be a better solution? But no matter. She places the receipt down onto the palm of your hand and then counts out the change. "That's five, ten, fifteen, twenty, thirty, forty, fifty, sixty, seventy, eighty, ninety and one hundred."

"Hundred dollars!" Randy reacts with both laugh and scoff. "You police do get paid good."

"Actually," you begin, the clarification of your employment on the tip of your tongue. But instead you seal your lips and tightly smile, nodding your head once. "Okay," you concede and put the change in your wallet before walking away from the register, feeling like a free man.

"Wait! You left something," Taryl then says from down the aisle and you turn around. She's holding up a piece of paper and it looks like a bill. Did you leave one of your tens?

"What is it?"

"It's your 50% off voucher."

"Oh," you expected something much more vital and exciting. She's only a few more steps away, but is it worth your while getting the voucher?

Are you really ever going to return to buy another sandwich after this entire ordeal?

Yes, you probably will. It would be 50% off.

You nod and complete the short journey back to the register and take the paper voucher from her. "Thanks."

"What's that for?" Randy asks as if annoyed. Clearly he wants one too.

"There was a hair in this sandwich," you say, holding up the package. "It's a bit of remuneration, I guess."

"It wasn't in *that* sandwich," Misty calls from her desk just behind you. "I grabbed you a new one."

"I just meant it was in the sandwich I bought."

Randy nods with a mischievous grin. "So what you're saying is, if I find a hair in my food, I get a coupon?" He looks at the lone item in his thick and calloused fingers: a package of Sesame Snaps. At first you think this to be a strange purchase for someone perhaps homeless, but then realize that they are high in calories and would actually be quite a prudent choice for someone on a limited income. Well done, hobo.

"You're not going to find any hairs in that," Taryl says to Randy.

"I might. Could be inside the wrapper."

"Then it wouldn't be our responsibility. You'd have to write to the company that makes those."

"What company is that?" Randy asks.

"I don't know." Taryl shrugs. "Sesame Snap Corporation, I guess."

"I actually think they're made in Poland," you add.

"Really?" Taryl says, more surprised than someone really should be from learning of such a thing. Is Poland really such an unexpected location?

You nod, but both Taryl and Randy are watching you, expecting verbal confirmation. "Yeah."

"Why aren't they made here?" Taryl asks.

You assume this to be a rhetorical question and just shrug. But then again you notice that both Taryl and Randy are watching you. "Uhm, I'm not sure. Perhaps Poland is closer to the sesame crop?"

"What do you think sesame plants look like?" Taryl asks and you realize that you don't have a clue. It's rather embarrassing.

"I don't know."

"Huh." Taryl says. "Do you think it might be a tree?"

"It's a tree." Randy says with far too much assurance. "A sesame tree."

"I don't think so." you reply, tempted to take out your phone and Google it right here and now. But no. Your data-plan doesn't allow for any frivolous web research.

But Taryl takes out her phone, seemingly without any hesitation. "Here, let me check. How do you spell it?"

"S-E-S-A-M-E," you say, although now ashamed that this cashier seems to pay for a better data-plan than an esteemed pilot. Are you too cheap when it comes to mobile technology?

"Huh," Taryl nods, "It's just called a sesame plant. It's from Africa, it says. It looks like weed—I mean, a weed." She turns her phone to you. "Is that what you thought it would be?"

From what you can see, it looks like a basil plant—quite surprising, you have to admit. You would have expected something less leafy.

"Is Poland near Africa?" Taryl asks, "I think it is."

"Not really," you say, "Depends on what your idea of *close* is."

Randy winces as she holds the package of Sesame Snaps hardly an inch from his eye. "I think this one's no good. I need a new one."

"It's fine, Randy." Taryl says with another sigh, passing a quick disparaging smile your way. "Let me run it through."

Randy asks, "Can I have one of them coupons? I do like those ham sandwiches."

You're not sure what it is—in fact, you're not even sure why you're still standing there. But you decide to do something good. You can see that this destitute man would get a lot of joy out of that voucher in your hands, much more than you'd ever receive, and so you pass it over to him. "Here, you take it. I don't need it."

His eyes widen like a weary tourist finally noticing his luggage tumbling down the carousel. "Why, thank you—"

"Actually," Misty calls out again from the customer service desk, "You can't give him that. It's for you only."

"But can't I give it to this man?"

"He didn't purchase the sandwich. You did. The voucher is non-transferable."

"Really?"

Misty replies, almost smug. "If you read the back, it says so in the fine print."

"But how would anyone ever know? There's no spot for my name."

"But I'd know." Misty says with authority. "If you don't want it, I'll take it back."

You expel a great a sigh and turn around. "Okay, then."

"Hey!" Randy calls, "If you don't want the coupon, just drop it on your way out!" He then winks as if Misty and Taryl weren't paying attention.

Misty shakes her head. "I heard that."

"I don't care." Randy says.

"I won't accept it."

"Ha!" Randy laughs, "I'll go to another store. You're not the only supermarket in town."

It's strange: although somewhat repulsed by this man, you're also rooting for him. These voucher rules are absurd and in need of a revolutionary to lead the way. Is Randy that revolutionary?

You decide to find out. You drop the coupon on your way out and immediately Randy charges to scoop up the fallen paper. "Got it!" He shouts and jumps in celebration. The last thing you hear as you walk outside is Taryl demanding Randy for his money or the Sesame Snap goes back in the bin.

And then the door slides shut behind you.

You're outside. You're free. The bright sunlight blinds you a moment and you wince, blinking and squinting through the blurry haze. You take a deep breath and hold it in, finally free.

But then you smell something in the air, something burning.

Looking east, you then realize that the sky is scarred with a billowing streak of acrid black smoke from the direction of the airport. Dozens of sirens are wailing in the distance. Pulling out your phone, you realize that the ringer was off and that you have dozens of missed calls and messages. Ann alone has left almost a half-dozen terrified and frantic messages, all referring to the explosion at the airport. She fears for your life.

What happened while you were stuck in the supermarket? Well, that's a whole other story. Right now, you're overwhelmed with an immense and surreal sense of appreciation. You're alive. If you hadn't gone to the supermarket, you could very well be dead. "Huh," you say with a slow nod, figuring that you should call Ann immediately to reassure her before opening the wrapping to take a bite of the sandwich.

It tastes fantastic. Too many tuna-salad sandwiches are overloaded with gooey mayo (or worse, cheap salad dressing), but this has the perfect proportion of tuna to mayo to bread. And there are even a few diced red peppers in there as well. Just a little bit of crunch.

It just might very well be the tastiest tuna-salad sandwich you've ever had—and that's *not* just because it indirectly saved your life.

The End

■ ■ ■

No, enough time had been lost already—and something in your gut tells you that the seemingly simple and quick task of purchasing a packaged sandwich from the grocery store would actually take a lot more time than it should. And, really, how many calories did you need to consume in a day? You're not in basic training anymore. You drive to work. You sit in a chair for hours upon end. A single day with a few pretzels and nuts would serve you just fine. Carbohydrates and protein. Honestly, what else does a man need?

When you finally arrive at the airport, you're hardly late at all. It looks like you made the right decisions this morning as you approach the parking attendant and flash your identification badge.

"Good morning," the lady says.

You can't recall her name, or perhaps you never knew it in the first place. "Good morning."

"Nice tie," she says as the entrance gate lifts upwards, ushering you in.

"Thanks," you say while unconsciously gripping the knot with one hand and adjusting it. Yes. This was a good choice. People notice these things. It is an omen: it's going to be a good day of work.

The End

■   ■   ■

"Thanks," you say as you grip the ceramic mug and bring the lip of it to your nose to take a whiff. It smells promising, but really what can you tell? You have many talents, but none that involve your sense of smell.

Finally, you take a sip with a wide smile.

It's the cheap stuff. Damn olfactory sense—it's let you down, once again.

You wince and wish that you'd gone with your instincts and asked for a travel mug. Now you'd have to carry this around all morning and pretend to drink it in front of her. Really, you should just end this problem, here and now, and tell her to stop making coffee with Sarah's old grounds. Ann is standing right in front of you pouring that disgusting almond milk over her cereal. Why can't you say something? How can she take offense to this? She didn't buy it. Why would she care?

"Are you okay?" she asks.

■ What do you do? ■

Turn to page 86 if you tell her the truth about the coffee.

Turn to page 87 if you tell her a white lie about the coffee.

"Yes please. But could you pour mine into a travel mug?"

There's a moment of silence—perhaps hesitation—before she replies. "Oh, okay."

You swallow hard. Why was there that pause? Is she upset? Is she on to you? Does she know what this means?

Ann passes over your coffee. "Here you go."

"Thanks," you take it, trying to read her expression—always difficult when one's eyes are sunken and crusty. You take a sip and roll it over your tongue. It's the cheap stuff. And she seems to be watching you. "Tastes great. Thanks."

"You're welcome."

What comes next is obvious: on your way to the airport, you'll dump this crap and pick up a real cup of coffee from one of those drive-through vendors. But at some point you really will have to find a way to get rid of that massive can of *PREMIUM QUALITY* coffee. Ann takes her mug upstairs to the bedroom and the moment she's out of sight you open the freezer and grab the colossal tin, still some three-quarters full. Actually, after further inspection you'd better approximate it to be at five-eighths full. There are literally hundreds of cups of this terrible coffee waiting to be brewed, right here, in between your cold hands. It seems a crime to remain complicit any longer. You risked your life to help once-and-for-all liberate the people of Iraq twice—could you really allow Ann to continue brewing this low-grade coffee, day after day, while doing nothing about it?

■ **What do you do?** ■

Turn to page 76 if you 'accidentally' drop the can on the ground, spilling all of its contents.

Turn to page 77 if you leave it for now, figuring that it is too early in the morning for such plans.

Running more hot water, you close your eyes and relax. You try to remember the details of the dream: standing in the kitchen, sorting through the recycling, Ann slicing celery, Scott Bakula on the television selling used cars…

But then you feel it. First in your toes and then along your thighs. The water is no longer hot. The water is not even lukewarm. The water is now cold. You sit up and twist off the tap, annoyed not only with all this now useless bathwater, but more so by the fact that you'd run out of hot water so quickly. Did Ann shower in the downstairs' bathroom? Or is the boiler malfunctioning again? Either way, there was no salvaging this bath. Like complimentary alcoholic drinks on domestic flights, you just have to accept that it's over. You pull the plug from the drain and get up.

Wrapping a fine Egyptian cotton towel around your waist, you gently walk past Emma's room as to not rouse her and enter the adjacent office, waking up the computer with a shake of the mouse. The screen flickers into life, displaying a disorganized and yet neat array of icons before a photograph of Emma taken when you visited Epcot Center last spring. And although Ann regularly changes the desktop photograph, in a sense, they never change. They are always pictures of your daughter: sleeping, crawling, playing in the yard, waving to the camera, passed out on the couch, sitting on Santa's lap, dressed up at a birthday party, making a snow angel, playing soccer… You love your daughter, of course, but also wonder just when it will stop. And honestly, you fear you know the answer.

It will never stop.

You sigh upon the revelation: the computer desktop has become the realm of women. Why is this? Back in the eighties there were no women at all in your computer classes. They shirked everything to do with such technology. The computer was as feminine as a motorbike. How did it all change? Why do women suddenly feel as if they have a right to personalize computers as they see fit? Perhaps it is time for you to take a stand… to liberate the desktop from years of maternal quirks and desires?

■ **What do you do?** ■

Turn to page 97 if you change the desktop to a photograph involving a scantily clad woman.

Turn to page 98 if you let it go and just check your email.

You depress the white button (that seems strangely similar to a delicious Mentos candy) and the grumbling jets churn the water all around you. It's like sitting in a warm pool of 7-UP. You slide back and close your eyes.

"Don't you have to work today?" Ann then asks, standing by the sink again.

"Of course."

"Then why are you using the Jacuzzi jets?"

"It's relaxing."

"You're not going to be late?"

"I'll be fine."

Ann looks down to you, seems ready to speak her mind, but merely chuckles and grabs her toothbrush.

"What's that?" you ask.

"Nothing."

"No, you had a little laugh to yourself. What's that about?"

She's clearly debating whether or not to tell you. After a few more seconds she says: "I just find it funny, how you, a military man and all, enjoy having a bath."

"What do you mean?"

"Having a bath—it seems feminine."

Of course you've heard this before, the strange cultural stigma associated with grown men taking baths. Even in the air force, when you'd risen to the top and demanded respect from all your peers and superiors, they still ribbed you for choosing to unwind in a bath after a long and dangerous mission. It didn't make sense; these same men would admit to looking forward to having a beer with their mates in a hot tub. But alone, somehow it was deemed girlish? The irrationality of it all made you furious.

■ What do you do? ■

Turn to page 73 if you attempt to debate Ann's point about taking a bath being inherently feminine.

Turn to page 75 if you let it go and get out of the bath.

"Ann," you say loud enough to be heard over the running water. "Could you come in here?"

She enters, her eyes bagged and heavy like a passenger departing a red-eye flight. "Yeah?"

"Did you notice this?" You direct her towards the deficiency with a nod of your chin.

"What?"

You almost want to scoff. This is exactly why she shouldn't *help* out with painting—she has no eye for detail. "That line."

"Where?"

"Just below the medicine cabinet."

She rubs her eyes and blinks. "What are you talking about?"

"Right there." Finally, you run your finger along the offending streak. "I just noticed it now."

"Oh. Yeah. I've never seen that. What do you think it is? Was it scratched?"

"No. I don't think it was painted properly."

She stands back up and seems both unconcerned and unimpressed. "Really?"

"Yeah."

"Well, I guess it's not a big deal. Neither of us noticed it before." She walks back out of the bathroom, closing the door behind her.

The medicine cabinet mirror is starting to fog up and you need to hold your fingers underneath the water for only an instant to realize that the desired temperature has been met. The morning shower awaits and you hope that it can wash away your sudden ire. And yet you can't just drop it so easily. Left alone, that streak of white will burn in your thoughts for the rest of the day. It might even affect your ability to navigate an airplane. People's lives would be at stake. Is it worth the risk?

There's a used can of paint in the crawlspace. You could get it, ready a brush, and paint over the affected area in less than five minutes. It would seem strange to Ann, but right now you're not really too concerned about what she thinks.

Or you could just take that shower like you originally planned.

■ **What do you do?** ■

Turn to page 69 if you decide to take the shower.

Turn to page 70 if you decide to paint over the streak right now.

There's no point getting into this now. Asking Ann about it would only make her defensive. It would taint the entire morning and you'd end up leaving on a sour note. You'll be a good husband and wait until after dinner to bring this up. You have plans for the evening; it won't matter if she gets in a foul mood.

Besides, you've waited long enough for that shower—and the moment you step underneath the cascading torrent of warm water, all your concerns about that poorly painted wall seem to vanish like bubbles in a freshly poured glass of 7-UP. If only you hadn't hit the snooze button, then you could have had the time to take a bath, to savor this for an extra nine minutes.

But no. You made your decisions. And now you'll have to live with them. Life is tough, but fair.

You grab the bottle of shampoo and squeeze a dollop onto your right hand before massaging it into your curly black hair. After more than twenty years of the mandated military buzz-cut, you've enjoyed letting your hair grow out a little. Running your strong fingers through your scalp, you wish that you could hire someone else to do this—your favorite part of getting a haircut having always been when the stylist washes your hair at the start. There's something about having a pair of confident-yet-delicate feminine fingers running through one's hair; it's a poor man's massage, if you will.

Now, speaking of massages, you think back to those ones in Thailand that you abided in while on leave in South-East Asia. *That* was a massage, you think with a chuckle, wishing that hair salons could offer such gloriously happy endings.

But that was the past. This is now. Rolling your head around under the showerhead, you rinse away the frothy lather and run your hands through your locks. It feels lighter. It feels clean. But can you do better?

■ What do you do? ■

Turn to page 99 if you use another dollop of shampoo.

Turn to page 100 if you move on to the conditioner.

Turn to page 101 if you decide instead to continue reminiscing about those Thai massages.

You pick up the buttermilk and take in a big whiff from the open spout. It smells worse than an airplane's economy restroom after a trans-Pacific flight—rotten cheese, vinegar, and a hint of body odor. You gag and wonder if it's gone off. How could Ann ever use this crap in baking? Granted, that banana bread she makes with it is quite tasty—but much of the credit for that deserves to go to the chocolate chips that you're always having to convince her to add. What does the buttermilk do? Perhaps you'll ask her to make it without the buttermilk next time, see how it tastes. It would have to be better.

Anyhow, you put the container of buttermilk back into the fridge, thankful that you didn't just pour it in without thinking.

Turn to page 68.

Another desire quashed by Ann's lack of forethought. Wasn't she just at the supermarket a few days ago? Why no 2% milk? Even on a domestic flight they have an adequate amount of milk on hand—and that's in economy class. Are you living in an economy style home? No way. It was time to make a stand. It was time to lay into Ann. You march to the bottom of the stairs, fold your arms and then call out: "Ann!"

"What?" She appears from the bedroom with a fine white Egyptian towel wrapped over her head. "And don't yell. You'll wake up Emma."

She's right. You shouldn't have been so loud. You reply with a throaty whisper: "We need 2% milk added to your weekly list."

"Okay." She shrugs. "I'll put it on the list."

"We're out."

"Of the 2%?"

"Yes."

She shakes her head while descending the stairs, "Is that all?"

You nod. "That's all."

"Why don't you try some of my almond milk?"

Almond milk—how can you even milk an almond? Is it not really just watery almond paste? What is that stuff called? Marzipan? You hate marzipan, so why would you somehow enjoy anything in the same food-family? It's almost as disgusting as that rice milk that you're seeing more and more in grocery stores. Is it not just the starchy run-off that normal people deposit down the drain after cooking rice? Are these people going to start marketing 'spaghetti milk' next? 'Potato milk'?

And then you see Ann pouring her almond milk over your cornflakes. It's an abomination.

"Here, just try it. I guarantee that you'll like it."

■ What do you do? ■

Turn to page 81 if you proceed to eat the cereal.

Turn to page 83 if you proceed to 'stumble,' knocking the bowl to the ground.

Thankfully, you find the shower exactly as invigorating as a pre-flight safety video is not—the moment you step underneath the cascading torrent of warm water, all your concerns about that poorly painted wall seem to vanish like bubbles in a freshly poured glass of 7-UP. If only you hadn't hit the snooze button, then you could have had the time to take a bath, to savor this for an extra nine minutes.

But no. You made your decisions. And now you'll have to live with them. Life is tough, but fair.

You grab the bottle of shampoo and squeeze a dollop onto your right hand before massaging it into your curly black hair. After more than twenty years of the mandated military buzz-cut, you've enjoyed letting your hair grow out a little. Running your strong fingers through your scalp, you wish that you could hire someone else to do this—your favorite part of getting a haircut having always been when the stylist washes your hair at the start. There's something about having a pair of confident-yet-delicate feminine fingers running through one's hair; it's a poor man's massage, if you will.

Now, speaking of massages, you think back to those ones in Thailand that you abided in while on leave in South-East Asia. *That* was a massage, you think with a chuckle, wishing that hair salons could offer such gloriously happy endings.

But that was the past. This is now. Rolling your head around under the showerhead, you rinse away the frothy lather and run through hands through your locks. It feels lighter. It feels clean. But can you do better?

■ **What do you do?** ■

Turn to page 99 if you use another dollop of shampoo.

Turn to page 100 if you move on to the conditioner.

Turn to page 101 if you decide instead to continue reminiscing about those Thai massages.

You didn't get to this point in your life by shirking from making those hard decisions at difficult times. There was that time in Kosovo when you were given orders to fire your Tomahawk missiles even though—but there's no time to get into that. Right now that defective streak of paint is an affront to your good taste and success in life. You twist off the water and descend the stairs. Ann is noticeably surprised to see you out of the shower and that's before you carry on to the basement, gathering painting supplies in your underwear.

"What are you—are you going to paint that spot right now?"

"Yes. I figure it should only take a few minutes."

Her mouth opens, a breath escapes, but then nothing more. Her face contorts through an array of expressions before she shakes her head and mutters, "Whatever."

You collect all that you need: the half-used can of Shaker Beige paint, a one inch bristled brush [unused and still in its packaging (thankfully you didn't return it to Home Depot, as was your usual post-renovation routine)], a ragged but cleaned blue rag, and a screwdriver.

A minute later and you're back in the bathroom, now prying open the can. Pulling back the lid, the gelatinous dribbles of paint look disturbing similar to what you seen when you open your mouth first thing in the morning. You slowly and delicately dip the flat tip of the brush through the thick surface of the paint and then back out, smearing the edge against the paint-covered rim of the can. This is it. You guide the brush to the wall and press it along the white streak, your motions as controlled and careful as when you are landing a 737 (although, really, modern airplanes pretty much land themselves; the passengers don't need to know that, however). After just a single stroke, the offending whiteness is gone. You unroll a few sheets of toilet paper and place the brush down atop. Success.

Unfortunately, like all success in life, this feeling is inevitably followed by a sense of vacancy and lament. What now?

■ What do you do? ■

Turn to page 71 if you get going with that shower.

Turn to page 72 if you take a moment to appreciate your handy-work.

THE MOST BORING BOOK EVER WRITTEN

You've successfully made your home a better place and helped it reach its full aesthetic potential. Now it's time for you to help yourself reach your full hygienic potential. You twist the shower's knob, pleased that you've done something significant so early in the morning.

Turn to page 69.

Is it really that boring to watch paint dry? Well, it's time to take that cliché head on. You stare at the glossy stroke, bold and brazen like a transatlantic flight in the fifties, and within seconds you feel the first squirming pangs of boredom—but you know this might actually be a good test for your mental stamina. You will not relent. You are a soldier.

After a few minutes and endless mind wanderings, a cramp develops in your thigh, forcing you to rub it a bit. Maybe it's dry now? You are tempted to reach out and touch—but what if it's not dry? Your gut screams no. Too risky. Like mowing the lawn without safety goggles or first applying sunscreen with a PH less than 30. *PH?* Is that even the right term? You're sure it's not and yet nevertheless refuse to check the moisturizer in the drawer to confirm. That's not why you came here.

Back to the paint, you tell yourself, leaning forward so close that you can smell the fumes and discern the individual bristled ridges of glistening paint. You watch for at least another minute, careful not to disturb the drying process with your exhalations. You would have hoped to have observed something by now. After all, you have an exceptionally keen eye for small details, honed from years in the military. And yet you notice nothing. It looks exactly the same as before.

But then, you do see something: a tiny ridge, like a single strand of hair, merges into an adjacent line to become one. It's like reverse mitosis. Or you think that is the term. Biology class was a long time ago.

■ What do you do? ■

Turn to page 85 if you continue to watch in case something else happens.

Turn to page 84 if you leave the room with a sense of satisfaction.

"It's not feminine." You say, sitting up slightly, ready for so much more.

Ann jabs the toothbrush in and out of her mouth a few times while staring at you with a blank expression. She then nods. "Okay."

You're not sure what else there is to say. You didn't expect her to concede with such ease. She then spits out into the sink and sips some water right from the tap. "You should probably get going."

She leaves the room.

In a way, you're disappointed. You doubt that you've really changed Ann's perspective on male bathing. But at the same time, being naked in a bathtub is hardly the best environment for a man to argue his case. Of course, you've seen that the English wear those silly curly wigs when in court. How could that possibly be beneficial? You almost think that you'd rather debate someone naked than wearing some sort of ridiculous grey-haired costume. What do the English have to hide that they need such strange coverings? Are they really that pale and out-of-shape? It's a good thing you live in America, you think with gratitude while unplugging the drain and standing up.

Wrapping a fine Egyptian cotton towel around your waist, you gently walk past Emma's room as to not rouse her and enter the adjacent office, waking up the computer with a shake of the mouse. The screen flickers into life, displaying a disorganized and yet neat array of icons before a photograph of Emma taken when you visited Epcot Center last spring. And although Ann regularly changes the desktop photograph, in a sense, they never change. They are always pictures of your daughter: sleeping, crawling, playing in the yard, waving to the camera, passed out on the couch, sitting on Santa's lap, dressed up at a birthday party, making a snow angel, playing soccer… You love your daughter, of course, but also wonder just when it will stop. And honestly, you fear you know the answer.

It will never stop.

You sigh upon the revelation: the computer desktop has become the realm of women. Why is this? Back in the eighties there were no women at all in your computer classes. They shirked everything to do with such technology. The computer was as feminine as a motorbike. How did it all change? Why do women suddenly feel as if they have a right to personalize computers as they see fit? Perhaps it is time for you to take a stand… to liberate the desktop from years of maternal quirks and desires.

■ What do you do? ■

Turn to page 97 if you change the desktop to a photograph involving a scantily clad woman.

Turn to page 98 if you let it go and just check your email.

You sigh upon noticing the emerging rolls along your belly, realizing that you have grown soft—mentally, spiritually, physically—and time is far too valuable to waste in arguing the merits of having a bath so early in the morning. You would argue these merits over dinner.

Wrapping a fine Egyptian cotton towel around your waist, you gently walk past Emma's room as to not rouse her and enter the adjacent office, waking up the computer with a shake of the mouse. The screen flickers into life, displaying a disorganized and yet neat array of icons before a photograph of Emma taken when you visited Epcot Center last spring. And although Ann regularly changes the desktop photograph, in a sense, they never change. They are always pictures of your daughter: sleeping, crawling, playing in the yard, waving to the camera, passed out on the couch, sitting on Santa's lap, dressed up at a birthday party, making a snow angel, playing soccer… You love your daughter, of course, but also wonder just when it will stop. And honestly, you fear you know the answer.

It will never stop.

You sigh upon the revelation: the computer desktop has become the realm of women. Why is this? Back in the eighties there were no women at all in your computer classes. They shirked everything to do with such technology. The computer was as feminine as a motorbike. How did it all change? Why do women suddenly feel as if they have a right to personalize computers as they see fit? Perhaps it is time for you to take a stand… to liberate the desktop from years of maternal quirks and desires.

■ **What do you do?** ■

Turn to page 97 if you change the desktop to a photograph involving a scantily clad woman.

Turn to page 98 if you let it go and just check your email.

"Oh no! Ann! Something terrible has happened."

"Oh my Gosh," her steps thunder down the stairs like tumbling luggage. "What! What? What?" she exclaims, walking into the kitchen as you point at the fallen can. All of its contents, even the smallest of granules, are on the floor.

"The coffee. I spilled all those grounds that Sarah brought over."

"Oh." She clearly expected something more dramatic, her chest still heaving. "But why are they all wet?"

"It's the craziest thing. I was drinking a large glass of cool, fresh Tropicana orange juice when I opened the freezer door and the coffee can tumbled out, knocking my juice all over them as well."

"Why were you going into the freezer?"

"I was thinking of taking out a steak for dinner tonight."

"But it's Wednesday. You know we have pork tenderloin."

"Oh, yeah. I was thinking it was Tuesday."

"Well," Ann shakes her head, "You'll need to clean it up."

"The punishment fits the crime. Again, I'm sorry." Although you try to grimace, inside you celebrate and a smile creeps across your lips.

"At least mix it in the garden," Ann adds before going back up the stairs. "It will be good for the perennials."

No it won't, you think; it's much more likely to kill them. "Oh, I was thinking I could just use the vacuum."

"What? At this time in the morning? Are you crazy? You'll wake up Emma. I'm surprised you haven't already with all this clatter. No, just sweep it up. And then you can put it in the garden. The grounds are good for it."

You know you're not going to win the battle of the vacuum, but you're definitely not going to torture your beloved parsnip patch, either.

■ What do you do? ■

Turn to page 88 if you insist on putting the grounds down the garbage disposal.

Turn to page 89 if you only pretend to put it in the garden.

Knock over the entire mammoth can of coffee? What are you thinking? The mess would take several minutes to clean up with all those grounds getting stuck between the tiles... Although you do figure that you could use the vacuum... and then it actually wouldn't take very long at all. In fact, it would hardly even take a minute to make the kitchen spotless. And looking down to your feet, you then notice a whole horde of things collecting in the grout: a raisin, a dried pea, what looks like a couple of rolled oats, and a few black hairs. You're revolted. This kitchen of yours is a sty. How can you live like this? You put down the can of terrible coffee, intent on getting the vacuum cleaner.

But then you figure if you're going to vacuum the floor, why not dump out the coffee grounds as well? You know, kill two birds with one stone...

Turn to page 76.

"Don't worry about it," you lean down and kiss her on the cheek. "Daddy's got to get going."

"Bye, Daddy."

Looking at the time, you're pleased to see that you're early, figuring that you'll get a leg up on the traffic. You wave goodbye to Ann as she checks her email and hurry down into the dark and cavernous garage. Punching the illuminated plastic button, you wait for something to happen.

But nothing happens.

The garage door doesn't open.

You sigh and press the button again—bemoaning the time and hassle that will surely be required later this evening to remedy the problem.

But the garage door opens. You must have just not pressed the button hard enough the first time. That was close.

As the door lifts and bathes the garage in the bright light of morning, your eyes immediately gloss over your own black Volvo sedan towards the gleaming chrome Jaguar XKR just to its side. It isn't yours, of course. The Jaguar belongs to your old military friend Carlos who asked you to take care of it while on operation overseas. It is a beautiful car—sleek, modern, expensive, and entirely impractical. You shake your head for a moment, wondering why Carlos would spend his money on such a trophy car... but then figure that he'd never know if you took it out for a spin. Really, what was stopping you from driving his Jaguar to work today?

■ What do you do? ■

Turn to page 16 if you decide to take Carlos's Jaguar to work today.

Turn to page 17 if you decide to take your own Volvo, as usual.

You: "What's a bowtie? It's a thing some men wear around their neck."

Emma: "What it look like?"

You: "Uhm, it's two triangles with a circle in the middle."

Emma: "What?"

You: "Okay. I guess you haven't learned your shapes yet. I'll have to talk to your pre-school teacher about that. Maybe, think about that pasta we eat sometimes."

Emma: "Pizza?"

You: "No, pizza is not a pasta. Noodles."

Emma: "P'sghetti?"

You: "No, not spaghetti. I think we had it a few weeks ago. The one that looks like... a bowtie? Crap, that's not going to help."

Emma: "You said a bad word!"

You: "No, I didn't. I said carp."

Emma: "What's carp?"

You: "A type of fish."

Emma: "Can we have fishsticks for dinner?"

You: "No. Today we have pork tenderloin. Fishsticks for lunch on Saturdays only."

Emma: "You have a bowtie?"

You: "No, no I don't. I don't believe in them."

Emma: "Why?"

You: "I think they look silly."

Emma: "What do it look like?"

You: "I think we've tried this already. Oh! I know... Mommy puts them in your hair sometimes."

Emma: "Pigtails?"

You: "No, not pigtails. A man couldn't wear pigtails around his neck."

Emma: "That would be silly!"

You: "Yes, yes. Very silly."

Emma: "You're silly, Daddy."

You: "Yes, yes. I know. You've told me that."

Emma: "Can I have bowtie?"

You: "But you don't even know what it is?"

Emma: "What is it?"

You: (silent groan)

Turn to page 78.

You've done a lot of crazy things in your life: flown into enemy airspace without permission, slept with six Malay prostitutes at the same time, even killed a man with your bare feet... and, yes, all of that was in your twenties, but who's to say that your wild days are behind you just because you're forty? You grab the bowl and thank your wife. You're going to eat those cornflakes with almond milk.

But first you let it sit a little longer just to make sure the flakes are good and soggy.

"You look nervous," Ann jokes when she walks past again. And fair enough. You've been standing in the middle of the kitchen with a bowl of cereal in your hands for a couple of minutes.

It's time. You hold the bowl with your left hand and pilot the stainless steel spoon with your right, scooping a dripping heap of limp flakes up to your lips. You hardly have to chew. The mushy cereal slides down your throat like oatmeal. You run your tongue over your teeth. You swallow again. And then you make your deliberation.

It tastes good.

The almond milk's sweetness lends itself quite nicely to the cereal. And it has a similar body to the 2%. When Ann returns, now dressed, you're scraping away the very last remnants on the bottom and sides of the bowl.

"I guess you must have liked it."

"I did," you say with no attempt to disguise your surprise.

"Well, I knew you would."

"Yeah," you say, putting the bowl into the sink and rinsing it out. As strange as it may sound, eating your cornflakes this morning with almond milk was enlightening. If you were so wrong about something as simple as almond milk, what else have you been wrong about for all these years? Is Sprite actually a respectable substitute for 7-UP? Could electric cars really prove to be enjoyable to drive? Might quinoa be a suitable substitute for rice at dinner? Was the war in Iraq not really about securing world peace?

Of all the things that you held true and dear to you, of all the things that you *knew*—did they mean anything?

You feel both emptied and liberated, and you're not sure how to react. On your drive to work, you don't listen to the radio, instead preferring the company of your own thoughts. As you approach the airport and then hold up your identification badge, you figure that you're going to keep doing the unexpected. Perhaps on today's flight you'd tell a joke over the intercom. Or announce your altitude in metric. Or proclaim your true feelings to Sandra, the head-steward.

Well, maybe not that last thing.

The End

■   ■   ■

"Thanks," you say, accepting the bowl of cereal with one hand and clasping the spoon with the other. "It looks great."

You're not sure how to pull this one off. You don't think you've ever dropped a bowl of cereal or soup before in your life—after all, you've made your living thanks to steady hands and a confident grip. But then Ann turns away and you realize that now is the time; it doesn't matter what reason you'll come up with. You part your hands and watch the bowl descend…

…But then, somehow, impossibly, amazingly, Ann spins and catches the bowl in mid-air right before your knees. The almond milk sloshes but doesn't spill. Not even a single drop. She exhales and stands back up, once again offering the bowl of cereal. "That was close. What happened?"

"I don't know. It just… slipped out of my hands."

"Well, it's a good thing I caught it. That would have been a horrible mess."

"Yes. Horrible."

"Here. You can take it now."

For the second time now, you accept the strangely persistent bowl of cornflakes and almond milk. "Thanks."

Turn to page 81.

Two words immediately spring to your mind:

Mission accomplished.

You carry the painting supplies down to the kitchen, placing the can and wet brush onto some unfolded newspaper. You know that Ann will expect you to put away these supplies but you decide to leave them there for the time being. Really, it should be her job—you're the one who cleaned up her mess, after all. And you really don't feel like putting it back into the crawlspace. It's so cramped down there. It's bad for your back. Ann is the one who does all that yoga, anyhow. She's flexible.

Yes, it's not your responsibility.

With a click of the remote, your widescreen television hums, pauses and then blazes into life, displaying some ridiculous cooking show where a man with too much gel in his hair is talking about avocados with the sort of reverence appropriate for something as tasty as parsnips. Ann always leaves it on one of those cable food networks—you wouldn't mind if she then transferred some of these skills into her cooking, but instead she just watches mindlessly. Are cleaning shows soon to become the next trend in reality television? Celebrity maids? Is there going to be a Homecare Network? Or does such a thing already exist? You have hundreds of channels on digital cable, so the chances are actually quite likely. It's a sad reflection on the state of modern society that there is a major television station devoted to cooking but not aviation. You press the guide button to change the channel to the local morning news, hoping to get the inside scoop on the local traffic situation before heading out the door. But then you wonder, which morning news channel will you turn to?

■ **What do you do?** ■

Turn to page 113 to turn to channel 211: *The Breakfast Show with Tina Gables and Darren Wilks.*

Turn to page 115 to turn to channel 209: *The Sunny Morning News with Sophie Chan and Glen Wilson.*

Resting your chin in the palms of both hands, you continue the grueling observation, breathing slowly and quietly as if meditating. Ann walks past the bathroom, her footsteps creaking along the floors, and you pray that she doesn't enter, that she doesn't ask you what you're doing. Because you're watching paint dry. She wouldn't understand. Really, you aren't sure if you have any friends or associates who might appreciate what you are delving into at this moment. This is uncharted territory. You are flying into the danger zone.

But nothing is happening. Those ridges of wet paint aren't losing their luster; they won't buckle or wrinkle. It is as if time has stood still. The universe has come to a stop. There's an itch on your right nostril and you scratch it with your little finger, careful not to let it slip inside. You hate it when people pick their nose. Even alone, secure behind a closed door in a room well equipped with anti-bacterial soaps and cleaners, you wouldn't do such a thing. Your mother taught you well.

Okay, you accept. There is nothing more to see.

Turn to page 84.

It's time to tell the truth. "No, Ann, things are not okay."

"I know," Ann quickly replies, much to your surprise. "You don't need to say it."

"Oh. Then you're not upset?"

"Why should I be? It's not your fault."

"True," you say in relief. This worked out perfectly. Too perfectly.

Ann turns around and fumbles around in the drawer, pulling out a rattling orange pill container.

"Diarrhea medication?" you ask in surprise.

"No need to drink the coffee. It will only make it worse," she guides your mug of coffee down to the counter.

"Sure."

She sighs, "How bad is it this time? I told you not to eat all those chicken wings last night."

"It's not too bad." Not the chicken wings—she'll think they're causing you bowel issues. The tradition of going out for Tuesday night wings is perhaps your most cherished ritual, and now Ann will ride you every time you eat them. This was turning into a terrible morning. "I actually think I might be okay."

"Yeah, you keep telling yourself that." Ann shakes her head dismissively as if you're an irresponsible little boy. "Here, take a few. This should tighten things up," she smiles while passing you four horse-sized pills.

■ **What do you do?** ■

Turn to page 90 if you attempt to tell the truth once again.

Turn to page 91 if you ingest the pills.

You quickly counter: "No, I'm fine."

"Is the coffee okay?"

"Oh yeah."

Ann pauses as if to read your mind. "You sure?"

"Of course. Why?"

"If you don't like it, you can tell me."

"But nothing's wrong."

"I mean, I guess I could have used the expensive stuff. I just used the coffee left over from Sarah's visit. I can't tell the difference, can you?"

Oh, how you want to speak your mind, to let it be known that her sister's cheap coffee has no place in your home. This is your chance to finally dispose of that mammoth tin. But would it be worth it? You know the answer and yet still you struggle with what to say next.

■ **What do you do?** ■

Turn to page 102 if you assure her that the coffee is good and that you can't tell the difference.

Turn to page 104 if you admit that the coffee is terrible and that you can most definitely tell the difference.

No way are these grounds going anywhere near your parsnip plants. You'd seen what damage this coffee could inflict. Just last weekend while you were making blueberry pancakes (as you did every Sunday), Ann brought over a cup of the swill—and when she wasn't looking, you dumped it into the aloe plant. Now as you look at it, hardly 72 hours later, the leaves are already as wrinkled and brown as senior citizens in PHX. If this is the effect it has on a plant, then what is this doing to your body? No, let the garbage disposal grind it into oblivion. With the speed of an F-16, you empty the aged Tupperware bowl into the sink, turn on the faucet and then hit the switch. The growling motor bursts into life, rattling the entire counter. But then there's the sound of grinding metal, a screech, a thud, and finally silence.

Shoot.

"What's going on down there?" yells Ann from the bedroom.

"Nothing," you respond instinctively.

"That sounded like trouble."

"It's fine."

A moment later, Ann is back in the kitchen with a tempered scowl across her face. "How many times have I told you not to put grinds in the sink?"

"A few."

"How about a thousand? I bet you've jammed it. I heard the ruckus from all the way upstairs."

"I don't know if it was really a *ruckus.*"

"Oh, it was a ruckus and now what are you going to do about it? First you spill all the coffee and now you jam the garbage disposal? Smart. Really smart."

"Well if the coffee was…" You stop in mid-phrase and drop it.

"You are not leaving until you either fix it or call a plumber."

You grimace; either way there will be a cost. Time or money.

■ What do you do? ■

Turn to page 93 if you choose time and try to fix it yourself.

Turn to page 94 if you choose money and call a plumber.

You sweep the coffee into its plastic Tupperware coffin, making sure to seal the lid as tight as an airplane's emergency exit. This coffee will never escape again. You've heard that it takes ten thousand years for plastic to biodegrade. Good. Then that should keep the world safe of these accursed grounds for just long enough.

You walk through the back patio door and are immediately struck by the crisp air and bright sky. You breathe in deep and hold it there a moment with your eyes closed, the sun already warm on your cheeks. Your neighbor, Roger Wang, is mowing his lawn and you can smell the freshly trimmed grass. A slight breeze blows past and ruffles your hair. You exhale, your lips closed and gently smiling. Somehow, you just *know* that it's going to be a wonderful day.

And then you hurl the Tupperware over the railing, over the back fence, and into the unkempt and undeveloped lot just adjacent to you.

You walk back inside, closing the door behind you.

"You put them in the garden?" Ann asks from up the stairs in Emma's room.

"Yup. The Tupperware had a crack in it, so I threw it out. I hope you don't mind."

"Sure," she says. "And thanks."

"You're welcome," you say with a triumphant grin, the feeling of victory as sweet as a glass of 7-UP. Those horrid coffee grounds will never again ruin a cup of coffee in your household. It felt great to take charge of the situation—you may have retired from the military, but you were still fighting for what you believed in. Some things just don't change.

Standing in the middle of the dining area, arms folded with confidence, you realize that it doesn't matter what happens the rest of the day. You've already done something important. You've already made a difference. Tomorrow morning you're going to have a fine cup of coffee. You'll grind the beans yourself. A dark roast, perhaps. Something with body and spirit.

You nod and clap your hands. You can't wait.

The End

■   ■   ■

"No, no, please." you say, holding up your hands to stop her from bringing those pills any closer to you.

But she bats away your flimsy defenses. "You need them. It will make you feel better."

"But this has nothing to do with the wings."

She cocks her head and groans. "Oh what, are you going to blame Sarah's coffee then?" She forces out a curt laugh. "You think that's what's given you indigestion?"

What can be said? Your only reply is a simple exhalation, a deflating baloon. There is no place for the truth here. You will not win this round.

Turn to page 91.

You thank your wife as you accept the four pills, each larger than the peanuts that used to be offered as complimentary in-flight snacks before half the human race seemed to develop a life-threatening allergy to them (you lament the loss of the in-flight peanut; salted almonds just don't quite cut it, for some reason). "Are you sure I need four?"

"Better safe than sorry."

"Okay." For a moment you think of slipping the pills in your pocket when she's not looking—but she keeps looking. She pours you a glass of water and hands it over. "Thanks," you say again, wondering about what havoc this will wreak upon your system.

"C'mon," Ann says, now annoyed with your hesitation. "I don't need to tell you how terrible it would be to have diarrhea on a flight. Those restrooms are disgusting."

"You're right." You exhale while staring down upon the palm of your right hand and those four pink pills. Why is everything stomach-related the color pink, you briefly wonder before accepting that there's no time for such diversions. You throw back the pills and flush them down with a couple large gulps of water.

"There you go," Ann says and pats your shoulder. "Next time, just ask. You don't need to be so proud all the time. Diarrhea happens to everyone." She shakes her head and walks back to the stairs, stopping at the base to add: "And we probably don't need to go for Tuesday night wings again anytime soon."

"I don't think it was the wings."

"Well then, what else could it be?"

You struggle with how to reply, since there was nothing wrong in the first place.

"See?" she concludes, as if your lack of words was all the evidence she needed. She then walks up the stairs, leaving you alone in the kitchen as your stomach begins to quiver and twitch like a smoker departing a flight. This is not going to be good.

Within twenty minutes the ironically-caused-by-the-stomach-medication cramps become so piercing and intense that you're forced to turn around mid-commute and head home. You nestle back into bed with a groan, wishing for a pill to counteract the effects of overmedicating on diarrhea medication. But there is no such thing. You will just have to wait it out, hoping to get some sleep… wondering just when Ann will agree to go out for chicken wings on a Tuesday evening again.

The End

■   ■   ■

Sure, you have a generous salary. You can easily afford calling in a plumber. But this is not about the money. This is about the principle. You are a man who refuses to back down, to pass the buck, to take the easy way out. You've risked your life on more occasions than Ann could ever know and so now is no time to call a plumber, to get someone else to do what you are perfectly capable of dealing with yourself.

You start by flicking off the power to the device before opening the cabinet door and inspecting the plastic and metal underbelly. You shake it a bit and everything seems secure. There are no obvious signs of damage or loose wiring. Realizing that you're going to have to go in from above, you stand up and reach through the black rubber throat down to its jagged and corroded teeth. Blindly running your fingers along the jagged blades, you can feel the grit of the coffee grounds and scoop out a handful, throwing it down into the other sink. Then you go back in, almost elbow deep, scrounging your fingers into all the many nooks and crevasses.

But then you hear a strange humming buzz.

And then you feel something move.

And then the garbage disposal spins back to life at full speed, the blades chewing through your fingers, hand, wrist and forearm as effortlessly as a jet engine consuming a sparrow. You scream and pull back—and through the black rubber seal you withdraw only a mangled stump of bone, gristle and meat firing long pulses of blood onto the counter with each of your many manic heartbeats. And it's then that you realize that the garbage disposal was off *before* you flicked the switch mere moments ago…

…You shake your head and a shiver runs down your spine.

"What a horrible vision," you say to yourself, holding up your right hand and clenching the full five fingers.

"What's that?" Ann asks.

"Nothing." No, you can't chance anything. Without both arms, you'd never be able to fly a plane. And besides, you have a generous salary. You can easily afford calling in a plumber. No matter how small the risk, you won't let that accursed *PREMIUM QUALITY* coffee cause any more harm. Not to you at least.

Turn to page 94.

"Okay, I'll call a plumber," you concede and grab the phone. Luckily, you don't need to waste any time looking up a number—you remember this annoying-but-catchy jingle that's been playing on the radio all the time:

If it's clogged, don't touch it
If it's broke, we'll fix it
Just make a call and we'll be over
Dial 555 9284

(Granted, the melody is really what got stuck in your head, but you don't know how to read music and so there is no point in attempting to transcribe the musical notes.)

After three rings, there's a click and a young woman's overly perky voice on the other end says: *"Hi! You've reached Jack's Plumbing. All our lines are clogged right now, but one of our operators hopes to get things flowing again soon enough. Please hold the line."*

You sigh, unsure if you've ever been put on hold before for a plumber. How many people were enduring some sort of pipe-based crisis before eight in the morning? This didn't seem possible.

But you stay on the line, pulling out a stool from under the counter and taking a seat. Strangely, there is no music, there are no announcements, there's nothing at all on the other end. Is this normal? Is there not usually something to listen to—if for no other reason than to assure you that your call hasn't been dropped?

After a minute, you say: "Hello?"

No one replies.

Ann calls from the bedroom, "Did you make an appointment?"

"Still on hold."

There's a click. There's a sound. You're sure that someone is about to get your information and address.

But instead a song plays.

And surprisingly, it's one of your all-time favorites…

We'll be singing
When we're winning
We'll be singing

I get knocked down
But I get up again

You're never going to
Keep me down

Pissing the night away
Pissing the night away

He drinks a whisky drink
He drinks a vodka drink
He drinks a lager drink
He drinks a cider drink
He sings the songs that
Remind him
Of the good times
He sings the songs that
Remind him
Of the better times:

Oh Danny boy
Danny boy
Danny boy...

I get knocked down
But I get up again
You're never going to
Keep me down

Pissing the night away
Pissing the night away

He drinks a whisky drink
He drinks a vodka drink
He drinks a lager drink
He drinks a cider drink
He sings the songs that
Remind him
Of the good times
He sings the songs that

Remind him
Of the better times:

Don't cry for me, next door neighbor...

I get knocked down
But I get up again
You're never going to
Keep me down

We'll be singing
When we're winning
We'll be singing

When the song finishes, you wonder how much longer you'll remain on hold for.

■ **What do you do?** ■

Turn to page 116 to stay on the line.

Turn to page 118 to lie to Ann and tell her that a plumber is coming later on.

It is time to add a little spice to your drab office. A beautiful woman draped across your screen would add some fire—and maybe even inspire Ann to start wearing skimpy underwear again. And come to think of it, maybe it would also pressure her to stop wearing pajama bottoms around the house every evening? Yoga-pants would be acceptable. She could pull them off, you think. Just not anything flannel.

Maybe that should be the screen saver: a realistically attractive woman dressed in yoga-pants? The symbolism could be great. But more could be done. Ann's efforts in the kitchen had definitely been dwindling over these last few years. Wasn't it only last week you ran out of 2% milk for coffee and cereal? And wasn't it also last week that you had to vacuum despite coming off a long flight? Yes, there needed to be a kitchen in the photograph. A tidy one.

Now is there anything else?

A pastry. Preferably filled with whipped cream. Not a cheap jam-buster or something. When was the last time Ann brought home some quality pastries? Last week she brought home bran muffins, and yes, they helped make you more regular, but surely there was more to your life than good bowel movements?

With Google at your fingertips, you type: *attractive woman yoga pants tidy kitchen cream-filled pastry*

Amazingly, dozens of thumbnail pictures meeting your criteria appear on your screen and you select the very first one. Minimizing the browser window, you sit back and appreciate the image as if it is a piece of art: beautiful, powerful, inspiring.

And then Ann walks in.

■ What do you do? ■

Turn to page 105 to conceal the image.

Turn to page 106 to let Ann behold the new desktop image.

With the click of a button, you log into your joint email account (meandann@gmail.com), sadly lamenting the demise of your private address (aceofspaces1970@hotmail.com), which withered and expired several years ago from lack of use, for it was decided that there was no need for such things. Well, it was Ann who decided for you and you never put up a fight—her argument being that a couple has one mailing address, and so they should only have one email address. And this was not an argument that you could win; any hesitation on your part would have only made her think that you had something to hide. And you didn't. And you still don't. And yet you wish your old account was active, the one you set up when email was like 7-UP in the 1930's—something new, exciting and unchartered. Before text messaging or fear of viruses or even spam. Imagine that—a world of email before spam! When you would read *every* incoming message excitedly. When every message meant something.

You sigh.

This morning, you have no new messages in your inbox. None at all. But there are literally hundreds of messages in the junk folder. Perhaps aside from all the claims for penis enlargement, cheap Viagra, and UPS delivery failures, there is something real—someone real—trying to get a hold of you? Perhaps it is time to look through your spam folder?

■ **What do you do?** ■

Turn to page 110 to look through your spam folder.

Turn to page 112 to leave the office and get dressed.

Oh yeah. What a great move. It really lathers up well and you massage it deep into the roots, pleased with your instincts, knowing your follicles will thank you later.

Turn to page 100.

You squeeze out a generous heap of rich, creamy conditioner into the palm of your hand and massage the slippery lotion all over your scalp, letting it sink in for a minute before rinsing it out. Afterwards, your hair feels as slick and sculpted as the body of a jet.

But then you wonder: what is conditioner? In the commercials, they show how it fills in the cracks in your hair like some sort of follicle-putty, but that actually disturbs you. You pick up the bottle and squint to read the ingredients: *water, stearyl alcohol, dimethicone, behentrimonium chloride, cetyl alcohol, coconut oil-cocos nucifera, jojoba seed oil-simmondsia chinensis, fragrance, panthenyl ethyl ether, panthenol, lysine HCL, methyl tyrosinate HCL, histidine, disodium EDTA, sodium hydroxide, methylchloroisothiazolinone, methylisothiazolinone and benzyl alcohol.*

Aside from water and the word alcohol, you recognize nothing. You read again:

water, stearyl alcohol, dimethicone, behentrimonium chloride, cetyl alcohol, coconut oil-cocos nucifera, jojoba seed oil-simmondsia chinensis, fragrance, panthenyl ethyl ether, panthenol, lysine HCL, methyl tyrosinate HCL, histidine, disodium EDTA, sodium hydroxide, methylchloroisothiazolinone, methylisothiazolinone and benzyl alcohol.

This time you notice the word sodium. Salt. Maybe one more time and it will all make sense: *water, stearyl alcohol, dimethicone, behentrimonium chloride, cetyl alcohol, coconut oil-cocos nucifera, jojoba seed oil-simmondsia chinensis, fragrance, panthenyl ethyl ether, panthenol, lysine HCL, methyl tyrosinate HCL, histidine, disodium EDTA, sodium hydroxide, methylchloroisothiazolinone, methylisothiazolinone and benzyl alcohol.*

Nope, none of it makes sense. In fact, it scares you. These things could very well be the same ingredients as in jet fuel. This is madness. Shouldn't someone do something to stop this insane use of chemicals?

Then again, it does leave your hair silky soft. And if it really is dangerous, wouldn't the government step in?

■ **What do you do?** ■

Turn to page 107 if you choose to ponder the role of government safety legislation.

Turn to page 108 if you choose to turn off the shower and dry yourself.

Your favorite went by the name Tonya. She had the smoothest skin and the softest hands. And you think you were her favorite as well—yeah, she smiled for all of her guests, but when you came into her dark and musty room, it was genuine. There was something about the look in those eyes, so dark they were nearly black. Her gaze would linger on yours longer than it had to. When others came for a massage, she was doing her job. But when you came, she was having fun. You both were having fun...

Ann knocks quickly before opening the door. "Sorry, I just want to grab my toothbrush."

"Of course."

"Are you okay?"

"I'm fine."

"You look scared."

"I was just... somewhere else, I guess."

Ann grabs her pink toothbrush and then leaves, closing the door behind her again.

You decide that this is no time for lingering on the past. Not in a crowded house, at least.

■ **What do you do?** ■

Turn to page 99 if you use another dollop of shampoo.

Turn to page 100 if you move on to the conditioner.

"It tastes good to me," you say with a smile. "You know: coffee is coffee."

"Yeah," Ann nods. "I never believe it when coffee snobs say that they can tell the difference."

You swallow hard. "Yup."

"Actually," Ann has a little chuckle. "You'll find this funny. When Sarah brought this over, she wasn't sure if you'd like it. She thought you might be one of those coffee snobs."

Is *coffee snob* a common term? And are you indeed one of them? But now two lies deep into this hole of fallacies that you'd dug yourself, what else can you do but laugh and grin along? And moments later when Ann leaves the kitchen carrying her cheap cup of coffee, you feel defeated, for now she is surely going to start buying that *PREMIUM QUALITY* crap on a bi-weekly basis. Perhaps for the rest of your life you will be accosted, each and every morning, by the insipid and yet bitter twang of the cheapest coffee money can buy.

Is this what you went to war for?

With Ann in the shower, you sigh and then dump your coffee into the sink. When you get to the airport, you'll pick up a cup of something better. This will have to become part of your daily routine. You'll start leaving five minutes earlier to give yourself time. Five minutes a day for the rest of your life. Hundreds of hours, weeks of your life, stolen, wasted in line for a paper cup of coffee. Just like that, you've surrendered.

Accepting that your life has now irrevocably changed, you decide to waste no more time and get dressed and leave as quickly as possible. Sure, Ann will be temporarily annoyed to find that you've left in such a rush, but no matter. This is your life now.

And all along your commute, you can't help but feeling that you did the wrong thing—that you should have told the truth about her sister's coffee. Really, what good had it done to lie? Would it have not been better to just tell the truth once-and-for-all? Sure, there might have been an hour or two of awkward tension, but then, like the people of Iraq now, you'd be free. As you pull up to the airport and hold up your badge to the parking attendant, you nod to yourself in begrudging acceptance. Honesty is always the best policy. Lies only begat more lies.

The End

■   ■   ■

"Actually," you begin but then falter.

"You don't like it?" Ann asks before you have a chance to find the right words.

There's no going back now. "I can tell that it's the cheap stuff."

"Can you?"

"Yeah."

"Oh."

"It's not a big deal."

"Well, it's a big enough deal for you to tell me."

"I'm just being honest."

Ann nods and turns to get something from the fridge. You think she's going to say something more, but instead she just seems to be pouting— just as you were afraid she would.

So you then add: "It's not like you bought it, right?"

"I know," she nods and hums as if agreeing with you but doesn't say anything else before carrying her cheap cup of coffee out of the kitchen and up the stairs.

You shrug your shoulders and then dump the coffee into the sink. There's no point in being delicate any longer. And there's no point in hanging around the house any longer, either. As soon as you hear Ann go into the shower, you quickly get dressed and make sure to leave the house before she gets out. Sure, she'll be temporarily annoyed to find that you've left in such a rush, but hopefully she'll have calmed down by the time you return home in the evening.

But all along your commute, you can't help but feel that you did the wrong thing—that you shouldn't have told the truth about her sister's coffee. Really, what good had it done? Would it have not been better to just carry on with the lie until that tin of grounds had been exhausted? You could have even chosen to slowly dispose of the grounds down the garbage disposal when she wasn't around. As you pull up to the airport and hold up your badge to the parking attendant, you nod to yourself in begrudging acceptance. Honesty is not always the best policy. Sometimes a white lie is needed to keep things smooth.

The End

∎ ∎ ∎

In a hasty attempt to conceal the desktop image, you double-click on the first icon that you see.

"Hey—what's that?" Ann asks.

"What's what?"

"On the computer; what's with the Excel?"

"Oh, that. I just wanted to do a little bit of budgeting."

Ann looks a little closer and grimaces. "But it's empty."

"I know. I'm just getting started."

"At seven in the morning?"

"I had some thoughts while I was in the bathroom."

"What about?" Ann asks, either interested or attempting to call your bluff.

"Compound interest."

"Oh."

"I'm just thinking about how to set up my columns."

"I still don't get why you've decided to do this so early."

"The earlier, the better." You nearly scoff, "That's how compound interest works, you know."

"But..." Ann slowly shakes her head. "Whatever." And then she leaves the room, apparently having forgotten about why she came in here in the first place. You then wonder if she is going to start expecting you to take care of all the family finances from now on. For as long as you can remember, Ann has been the one who tallied all the bills, paid the credit cards, and organized everything. Of course you are perfectly able, but somehow it just became her responsibility. Will this change? Now that she thinks you're toiling over investment income in the early hours of the morning, will this become *your* monthly task? You groan, wondering what you'll say if this comes up. All because you thought of changing the desktop. What a mistake that was. You quickly go into the settings and revert the image back to the photo of Emma. Perhaps it's best to concede defeat in this battle: women shall continue their reign over the desktop background.

Feeling vaguely despondent, you remember why you came into the room in the first place: to check your email.

Turn to page 98.

There is nothing to hide here. With your arms folded you say hello while gently nodding your head, admiring your work.

"Hey—what's that?" Ann asks.

"What's what?"

"On the computer; what's with the picture?"

"Oh, that. I just wanted to change it up a bit."

Ann looks a little closer and grimaces. "Who is that?"

"I don't know. I just Googled it."

"Why is she holding a cream-puff?"

"I believe it's called a cannoli, actually. It's an Italian ricotta-filled pastry. It looks delicious, doesn't it?"

"It looks like she just came back from a workout. Why would she be eating something so fattening?"

"Maybe it's not for her? Maybe it's for someone else?"

"But it looks like she's about to lick it."

"Her kitchen sure is clean and tidy, isn't it?"

"It's a photo shoot. It's probably not even a real kitchen."

"But it looks good."

Ann slowly shakes her head. "Whatever." And then she leaves the room, apparently having forgotten about why she came in here in the first place. At this point, you can only hope the image affects her subconscious mind in some subtle manner. That she'll purchase sexy clothes the next time she's at the mall. That she'll pick up some cream-filled pastries the next time she's at the supermarket. That she'll keep the kitchen a little more tidy the next time she comes home in the evening.

Feeling pleasantly triumphant, you remember why you came into the room in the first place: to check your email.

Turn to page 98.

It should be stated that you are no fan of big government. You've always perceived yourself a self-made man, someone who doesn't ask for handouts, someone who doesn't need to be told what to do. (Unless, that is, when you were in the military. There you were told what to do all the time. And that was, in a sense, an extension of the government. But it was different. You're not sure how, but you know it was.)

And yet you also appreciate that companies need abide by some regulations. You've seen first-hand what happens when societies descend into anarchy. So, perhaps corporations are not able to self-govern? Perhaps there is the need for a corporate peacekeeper? Someone who dashes through the lavish lobbies of America's largest head-offices with baby blue caps and demands that the two sides drop their arms. Or litigations.

Are you even making any sense anymore? How did reading the ingredients on a bottle of conditioner lead to this ridiculous visual? Are you going crazy? Is this a sign of age, or spending too long in the shower, or of your vacant and meaningless existence?

Or is it because of all the chemicals in the conditioner that you've been rubbing into your scalp, every morning for the last thirty years?

You quickly rinse off your hair and body, hoping to flush away every trace of any possible chemical. Of course, isn't there still fluoride in the water? You remember some proposition a few years back to remove it and at the time you scoffed at the idea.

Did those sepia-toothed hippies have a point?

If only life was always as simple as it was back in basic training. Get up when they tell you to get up. Run when they tell you to run. Drop and give them fifty when they tell you to drop and give them fifty. You didn't have the time or energy to find yourself lost in such either vital-or-trivial thoughts.

And to think—in boot camp, you'd have already jogged a half-dozen miles by this time of the morning.

What had you done today?

Nothing. It was time to get out of the shower.

Turn to page 108.

You twist off the water and step onto the bathmat, grabbing your long, plush white towel made from the finest Egyptian cotton. You remember when Ann first bought these—you were absolutely irate when you saw the bill. Almost five hundred dollars for the set. It seemed obscene. How could someone spend so much money on a few towels? You figured that you could have used toilet paper to dry yourself off, if the need arose. It was a tense drive home, you not wanting to say a word to Ann. $500. Imagine how much 7-UP you could buy with that?

But then you used them. You'd never handled a towel so soft, so giving, so airy and light. You felt like you were suspended in the clouds when you dried yourself off after a shower. Suddenly, you didn't know how you'd ever used anything less. Ann was right: nothing compares to pure Egyptian cotton. Like Peruvian hardwood or Maldivian leather, it was one of the finer things in life.

You never told her this, of course. You just stopped harassing her about the expensive towel purchase, knowing this was praise enough.

As you descend the stairs, completing the last knot in your tie (you decided to go with a simple gray tie today), you grab the remote from the kitchen island and turn on the television. Your widescreen television hums, pauses and then blazes into life, displaying some ridiculous cooking show where a man with too much gel in his hair is trying to make feta cheese look sexy. You shake your head: there is *nothing* sexy about feta cheese. Ann always leaves it on one of those cable food networks—you wouldn't mind if she then transferred some of these skills into her cooking, but instead she just watches them mindlessly. Are cleaning shows soon to become the next trend in reality television? Celebrity maids? Is there going to be a Homecare Network? Or does such a thing already exist? You have hundreds of channels on digital cable, so the chances are actually quite likely. It's a sad reflection on the state of modern society that there is a major television station devoted to cooking but not aviation. You quickly change the channel to the local morning news, hoping to get the inside scoop on the local traffic situation before heading out the door. But then you wonder, which morning news channel will you turn to?

■ What do you do? ■

Turn to page 113 to turn to channel 211: *The Breakfast Show with Tina Gables and Darren Wilks.*

Turn to page 115 to turn to channel 209: *The Sunny Morning News with Sophie Chan and Glen Wilson.*

It is time to take out the metaphorical trash. Or is that personification? No, it is metaphor—and yet also literal. Perhaps you are going to take out the symbolic trash? Time to empty the virtual dumpster?

Message 1: *American Express special one time offer.*

Delete.

You use MasterCard Titanium exclusively.

Message 2: *Lose weight fast and safely with one pill.*

Delete.

Although not nearly as toned as you were when in the military, you are still in better shape than most men of your age.

Message 3: *I tested this meds shop out, check it out for yourself now*

Delete.

Not only are Vitamin D supplements the only pills you'll allow in your body, you don't trust the author's grammar. There really should be a period or semi-colon between those two clauses.

Message 4: *10 free Viagra pills. Order cheap Cialis plus many other generic pills*

Delete.

You have taken Viagra before, back when you were on leave in the Philippines. And while it sounded like a harmless endeavor for a man of your age, you proceeded to run the entire gamut of side effects: temporary color blindness (which is especially dangerous for a pilot), relentless headaches, and a disturbingly painful erection that lasted longer than three hours (which is especially dangerous for a pilot). It may sound funny, but it's not. You don't ever want to go through that again.

Message 5: *Am looking for my soulmate.*

This is from someone named Viky. You are briefly tempted… but…

Delete.

You don't trust someone with such a misspelled name.

Message 6: *$129 Replica Watches. Buy Cheap Replica Rolex Watches.*

Delete.

No need for a Rolex watch, replica or real. Your phone keeps perfectly good time and automatically updates when you fly between time zones. What Rolex does that?

Message 7: *Penis Enlargement Pills $59.95*

You laugh, or perhaps just scoff. The cursor lingers atop the trash button.

■ What do you do? ■

Turn to page 133 if you trash the penis enlargement email.

Turn to page 134 if you open the penis enlargement email.

You get up and turn off the monitor—but immediately wonder if it really matters. It's not 1990 anymore; these modern computers power down really quite quickly. How much energy were you really saving? A few cents a day... *at most*. In fact, you're probably causing more harm than good through all the wear-and-tear on the monitor's power button. Wouldn't *that* be terrible: if one day you can't turn on the monitor all because you thought you were doing something good for your wallet and the environment.

It's decided then: you will no longer turn off the monitor. The computer can make its own decisions.

With yet another big decision out of the way, you return to your bedroom and decide to get dressed. Looking through your closet, you accept that there really aren't many clothing choices for a pilot. Black slacks. White dress shirt. Black blazer with brass buttons and a few gold stripes. The only avenue for self-expression in a pilot's wardrobe comes from his tie—and you finger through the long line of neatly organized accessories, unsure of what you want today, what would relay your mood and character to the world. You certainly have a wide variety of choices: charcoal, pewter, silver, slate, steel, leaden, shadow, newsprint, dark gray, light gray... and just gray.

After much deliberation, you select two. But there can only be one.

Sometimes it seems that life would be so much easier *without* all these options...

■ What do you do? ■

Turn to page 13 if you go with the charcoal tie.

Turn to page 14 if you go with the dark gray tie.

Tina Gables is laughing at something that Darren Wilks said and you wish you had turned to this channel just a few seconds earlier. You always liked Darren Wilks—his friendly and unassuming demeanor made him seem like a neighbor, someone you would feel comfortable with walking over to and asking to borrow a power tool on a Sunday afternoon. Not that you would ever need to borrow anyone's power tools. You have more than enough. Just last month you purchased a chainsaw in order to take down a sickly tree in the backyard. How many people own a chainsaw? In fact, you're actually a little disappointed that none of *your* neighbors have ever come by to use any of your tools. Wasn't it last week that you saw Roger Wang coming home with a rented wet-saw from The Home Depot? Why didn't he just ask to use yours? Your wet-saw was far better than the flimsy and weathered thing that Roger ended up cutting tiles with. Perhaps it has to do with his Chinese heritage—they are a proud and reserved people. Probably not even allowed to borrow things from neighbors back in the motherland. It might be against the communist way of life. You're not sure. Perhaps you'd educate him on western neighborly ways the next time you saw him. Let him know that it's not a sign of weakness to ask for something in America. Unless that something is in the form of welfare. That is most definitely a sign of weakness.

"So, we're going now to Kaitlyn Hurst in the Taco Bell Trafficopter." Darren Wilks says, which immediately gets your attention. *"Kaitlyn, how are things looking up there?"*

The screen changes to the young and perhaps frightened Kaitlyn Hurst high above the city, holding her overhead microphone close to her lips. *"Thanks, Darren. I'm looking at the Johnston Hill interchange right now and traffic is really backed up due to an accident on the interstate. All four eastbound lanes are at a standstill right now with cars backed up all the way to exit 28. It is really ugly out here, and if you can avoid the area, please do. It doesn't look like it's going to clear up anytime soon. And the next time you have a hunger, drive over to your nearest Taco Bell to get their new Ultimate Combo Box. Tacos, burritos, nachos, fries and a soda all for only five dollars. From high above the Johnston Hill overpass in the Taco Bell Trafficopter, I'm Kaitlyn Hurst."*

Crap. Now you are craving some dirty Taco Bell. And the Johnston Hill area is right on your way to the airport. This is really going to mess up your morning commute.

■ What do you do? ■

Turn to page 131 if you decide to leave immediately and take the light-ridden route through the city.

Turn to page 132 if you decide to leave immediately but risk the freeway.

You turn to channel 209 only to see Sophie Chan and Glenn Wilson fading to black before a break. You're a busy man and there's no time to waste watching a complete cycle of commercials. Tina Gables and Darren Wilks, it is…

Turn to page 113

Much to your surprise, the same song starts up again. But you can't very well hang up now. Plus, you used to listen to this song all the time—why not a second time right now?

We'll be singing
When we're winning
We'll be singing

I get knocked down
But I get up again
You're never going to
Keep me down

Pissing the night away
Pissing the night away

He drinks a whisky drink
He drinks a vodka drink
He drinks a lager drink
He drinks a cider drink
He sings the songs that
Remind him
Of the good times
He sings the songs that
Remind him
Of the better times:

Oh Danny boy
Danny boy
Danny boy...

I get knocked down
But I get up again
You're never going to
Keep me down

Pissing the night away

Pissing the night away

He drinks a whisky drink
He drinks a vodka drink
He drinks a lager drink
He drinks a cider drink
He sings the songs that
Remind him
Of the good times
He sings the songs that
Remind him
Of the better times:

Don't cry for me, next door neighbor...

I get knocked down
But I get up again
You're never going to
Keep me down

We'll be singing
When we're winning
We'll be singing

■ **What do you do?** ■

Turn to page 120 to stay on the line.

Turn to page 118 to lie to Ann and say that the plumber is coming later on today.

Ann comes back down the stairs just as you hang up the phone. "So?" she asks, not needing to say anything else.

"Uh, yeah. The guy said he's going to come around later."

"Oh. When?"

"Five."

"This evening?"

"Sure."

"Will you be back around then?"

"No."

Ann sighs, "Well, I don't know if I can get back home at that time."

"That was the latest he could show up."

"Really? Five? Then you should have called a different plumber."

"I was on hold long enough as it is."

"Well, we have to get the garbage disposal fixed."

You then ponder Ann's last remark: do you really need to get the garbage disposal fixed? What does it really accomplish, flushing organic waste down the drain? Is it any better for the environment? Or is just for the fun of it? And when did the garbage disposal become a staple of middle-class life? Did people in the 70's see this coming? What other useless things will soon become commonplace in people's homes? An addition to the furnace that safely burns old magazines and papers? A second handle on toilets that allows one to shred and then flush down used shoes and boots? Maybe a backyard cannon that fires old oranges and other fruit into the air and out of sight?

Actually, that last one would be cool. You would be pleased if such a device existed—unless your neighbors had it as well. You'd definitely want to be the only house on the block with it.

"Well?" Ann says, obviously annoyed by your long stretch of pensive silence.

"I don't think we need to get the garbage disposal fixed."

"What do you mean?"

"Really, why do we need a garbage disposal, anyhow? When you think about it, they are ridiculous things."

Ann just stares at you as if expecting you to repent your sins. Then: "We're getting the garbage disposal fixed. Here," she grabs the phone. "I'll call the plumber."

You try to repress your smile. Although this was never part of the plan, it still feels that things have worked out in your favor. You agree and decide to get going before this conversation can continue any further, immediately hurrying up the stairs to get dressed.

■ **What do you do?** ■

Turn to page 127 if you aim to be on the road within five minutes (which is perhaps unreasonable).

Turn to page 129 if you aim to be on the road within ten minutes (which is likely more reasonable).

It can't be.

We'll be singing
When we're winning
We'll be singing

I get knocked down
But I get up again
You're never going to
Keep me down

Pissing the night away
Pissing the night away

He drinks a whisky drink
He drinks a vodka drink
He drinks a lager drink
He drinks a cider drink
He sings the songs that
Remind him
Of the good times
He sings the songs that
Remind him
Of the better times:

Oh Danny boy
Danny boy
Danny boy...

I get knocked down
But I get up again
You're never going to
Keep me down

Pissing the night away
Pissing the night away

He drinks a whisky drink
He drinks a vodka drink
He drinks a lager drink
He drinks a cider drink
He sings the songs that
Remind him
Of the good times
He sings the songs that
Remind him
Of the better times:

Don't cry for me, next door neighbor...

I get knocked down
But I get up again
You're never going to
Keep me down

We'll be singing
When we're winning
We'll be singing

Surely it can't play yet again?

■ **What do you do?** ■

Turn to page 122 if you stay on the line.

Turn to page 118 if you lie to Ann and tell her that a plumber is coming later on.

You're no longer sure if this is a good thing or not.

We'll be singing
When we're winning
We'll be singing

I get knocked down
But I get up again
You're never going to
Keep me down

Pissing the night away
Pissing the night away

He drinks a whisky drink
He drinks a vodka drink
He drinks a lager drink
He drinks a cider drink
He sings the songs that
Remind him
Of the good times
He sings the songs that
Remind him
Of the better times:

Oh danny boy
Danny boy
Danny boy...

I get knocked down
But I get up again
You're never going to
Keep me down

Pissing the night away
Pissing the night away

He drinks a whisky drink
He drinks a vodka drink
He drinks a lager drink
He drinks a cider drink
He sings the songs that
Remind him
Of the good times
He sings the songs that
Remind him
Of the better times:

Don't cry for me, next door neighbor...

I get knocked down
But I get up again
You're never going to
Keep me down

We'll be singing
When we're winning
We'll be singing

■ **What do you do?** ■

Turn to page 124 if you stay on the line.

Turn to page 118 if you lie to Ann and tell her that a plumber is coming later on.

We'll be singing
When we're winning
We'll be singing

I get knocked down
But I get up again
You're never going to
Keep me—

"Are you still on hold?" Ann asks as she walks past the kitchen to the front closet.

"They just keep playing *Tubthumping*," you say with a mix of shock and amazement. Mostly amazement.

"What's that?"

"You know? By Chumbawamba?"

She shrugs her shoulders. "I don't think I know the song."

"Trust me, you know the song."

"How does it go?"

You've always hated it when people ask you to sing a song. You fly planes. You don't sing. "You know. *Tubthumping*."

"I don't think I know it."

"Come here and listen."

Ann shakes her head as she returns to the stairs, "That's all right." She disappears from sight.

—Pissing the night away
Pissing the night away

He drinks a whisky drink
He drinks a vodka drink
He drinks a lager drink
He drinks a cider drink
He sings the songs that
Remind him
Of the good times
He sings the songs that
Remind him

Of the better times:

Don't cry for me, next door neighbor...

I get knocked down
But I get up again
You're never going to
Keep me down

We'll be singing
When we're winning
We'll be singing

■ **What do you do?** ■

Turn to page 126 to stay on the line.

Turn to page 118 to lie to Ann and say that a plumber is coming later on.

We'll be singing
When we're winning
We'll be singing

I get knocked down
But I get up again
You're never going to
Keep me down

Pissing the night away
Pissing the night away

He drinks a whisky drink
He drinks a vodka—

Okay, this is just too much. You love *Tumthumping* as much as the next heterosexual man, but *five times in a row?* That's like downing five cans of 7-UP in one sitting—truly, too much of a good thing. Not only would it be terrible for your teeth, your blood sugar levels would spike and then plummet. It is time to take charge of the situation.

Turn to page 118.

A quick exit is essential—the more you linger, the better her chances of pressing you about the whole plumber fiasco. Five minutes is not much time, but you've always been the type of person to thrive off a good challenge. Much like the promise of a flight arriving a few minutes early, it would be difficult, but not impossible.

0:00

Luckily you don't have a lot of options with regards to your wardrobe, the only variable being the color of tie. You grab the first one on the left. It's the gray one. It will do.

2:47

Completing the final folds and tugs of your tie as you leave the room, you need to say goodbye to Emma. She's just waking up and you give her a kiss on the cheek. "Love you," you say on the way out of the room.

"Daddy—"

"No time!"

3:14

You run back down the steps to the front foyer, scrambling to find your black leather shoes. Opening the closet, you're accosted by a bewildering array of Ann's footwear but seemingly none of yours. Why does someone need so many pairs of shoes? A 1:1 ratio of shoes to coats would—but then you shake your head. There's no time for these ponderings. You're running out of time.

4:18

You're forced to grab what you can, given the situational constraints: an old pair of brown walking shoes. And there's no time to put them on. Still in your socks, you scurry into the garage and pummel the button to begin raising the door.

4:47

You engage the engine and shift into reverse.

4:55

You gently depress the accelerator. The engine whirs. But nothing moves.

4:58

The emergency brake is still up! You depress the button and lock it down. The car rolls back.

But it's too late.

5:07

Turn to page 135.

Although there is hardly time to squander, ten minutes seems more reasonable. Your life is crammed with enough stress and deadlines as it is; there is no need to impose something as arbitrary and unrealistic as a five-minute getaway.

0:00

You saunter into the walk-in closet to piece together your ensemble for the day—not that there is much to choose from. A pilot's uniform is like a cold glass of 7-UP: clean, crisp and the same all over the world. And while there are a few options with regards to your tie, you end up going with the gray one. But then you hesitate. You also grab the slate tie. Would that be better? You hold each up to your neck and stare into the mirror's reflection. No. Stick with the gray.

4:12

Completing the final folds and tugs of your tie as you leave the room, you need to say goodbye to Emma. She's just waking up and you give her a kiss on the cheek. "Love you," you say while messing her hair with your hand.

"Daddy?"

"What's up?"

"Where you going?"

"I'm going to work."

"Can I come?"

"No."

"Why not?"

"Because you have to go to preschool."

"Why?"

"Because you have to learn things. Like," you pause and try to think just what it is students learn in preschool. Sharing? Finger-painting? Did they still have naptime? You weren't sure. Realizing that you really should take a larger role in your daughter's early childhood education, you decide to attend the next parent-teacher interview. But are they called teachers? Preschool teachers? It's really just daycare, isn't it?

And then you look at the time on your phone. "Never mind. You just have to go to school. Such is life."

"But Daddy—"

"No time!"

7:19

You run back down the steps to the front foyer, scrambling to find your black leather shoes. Opening the closet, you're accosted by a bewildering array of Ann's footwear but seemingly none of yours. Why does someone need so many pairs of shoes? A 1:1 ratio of shoes to coats would seem appropriate. A spring jacket and sporty pair of sneakers. A dinner jacket and a pair of high-heel shoes. A raincoat and rubber boots. That sort of thing—maybe throw in a couple pairs of sandals and you're good. But you estimate Ann's shoe to coat ratio as something closer to 4:1. That's just absurd.

Finally, you find your work black leather loafers beneath a pair of Ann's running shoes. She must have tossed them into the closet without thinking after going for a jog last night.

9:12

How did time escape you so? You pull open the laces and hastily cram each foot in before hobbling into the garage and pummeling the button to lift the groaning metal door. Ann is asking you something from the living room but her words remain unintelligible from the cool confines of the garage. You look at the time.

9:42

You engage the engine and shift into reverse. Victory is yours.

9:51

You gently depress the accelerator. The engine whirs. But nothing moves.

9:58

The emergency brake is still up! You depress the button and lock it down. The car rolls back.

But it's too late.

10:07

Turn to page 135.

There seems to be no choice. Even if the detour costs you as much as fifteen minutes, you would rather spend that time moving as opposed to idling under the increasingly bright sun of the morning. You tell Ann of the bad traffic news, give Emma a kiss just as she trundles out of bed, and hurry into your Volvo.

Avoiding the freeway means taking roads rife with long lights, slow busses, self-righteous cyclists and left-hand turning cars clogging scarce lanes. It's obscene. It seems to go against the very values of what it means to be an American. In a free country, why should you be forced to wait at those incessant red lights? And now the local transportation authority has begun to install those absurd traffic circles at intersections. *"It's European,"* the bureaucrats in charge always say as if that is an answer into itself. What the hell are you supposed to do with these? Traffic is meant to move in straight lines, not circles.

Just after navigating one of these strange roundabouts, you notice a supermarket to your right and realize that in your haste to get going you neglected to pack yourself a lunch. Having always been a fan of pre-packaged sandwiches, you ponder whether you have the time to purchase something. It's either that or procuring a bag of pretzels and almonds on the plane—these short-haul flights not even offering meals anymore. You don't really want to add any more time to your journey, but you also really don't want to have to subside on packaged snacks.

■ What do you do? ■

Turn to page 34 to stop into the supermarket for a sandwich.

Turn to page 57 to carry on to the airport, accepting the inevitable snack-sized lunch.

As much as it pains you to go against the wisdom of Kaitlyn Hurst, there really are no other options. And if there is any chance of you getting to work on time, you'll have to leave immediately. You tell Ann of the bad traffic news, give Emma a kiss just as she trundles out of bed, and hurry into your Volvo.

Much as you feared, the commute is wrought with peril. The four lanes of eastbound traffic bunch up and come to a halt before exit 21. It takes you ten minutes just to move a quarter mile according to your odometer. A man in a grey Subaru merges into your lane without signaling. Someone's stereo blasts bass-heavy hip-hop so loud that you can feel it in your seat. A woman in a red Honda Civic impatiently honks at you when you don't inch forward quickly enough for her liking. You have to turn on the A.C., which quickly dries out your skin (and you don't have any moisturizer in the car). You forgot your CDs and the radio seems to play nothing but commercials. The change-oil light comes on, which means another twenty bucks thrown down the drain (which is, incidentally, where you'll dispose of your used motor oil). You can't get a good signal on your cell phone when trying to call into work. Hardly a minute after switching lanes, you discover that you have to switch back. And no one wants to let you in. When you finally reach the accident—a Jaguar has been sliced nearly in half by a wayward flatbed truck—you're told to stop to let in a tow truck, holding you up for yet another couple of excruciating minutes.

When you eventually make it to the airport's staff parking lot and wearily hold up your identification badge to the attendant, you sigh and say, "What a terrible morning."

"Oh, what happened?"

"The traffic was terrible on the interstate. Took me forever."

"Oh." She almost seems disappointed but then smiles. "Well, I guess it's got to get better then, right?"

You nod in pensive acknowledgement. Yes, it certainly can't get any worse.

The End

■　■　■

Delete.

There are more messages, many more. Hundreds more. Even if you spend a measly ten seconds on each one, then this will still take you another half hour. And why? What is your life missing that can be filled via an unsolicited email message?

You click the 'select all' and then prepare to delete them all. Like dropping a bunker-buster, nothing will remain.

But you can't. Who knows what else might still linger in there? Maybe an old friend? Maybe that Thai masseuse you liked so much? There is no need to be hasty. Perhaps later on at night you will check these out more thoroughly. You can never be too sure.

Turn to page 112.

You're about to left-click the mouse.

But then you stop.

Just what are you thinking? Who knows what viruses might be sheathed in that message? And for what? You don't need assistance in that area. In fact, you're pretty darn certain that you're a little above average when it comes to such things (actually, you're not—in terms of both length and girth, your penis is exactly in the 50% percentile for adults).

Delete.

Message 8: *Ann, it's me. Ricardo.*

You chuckle at this strange coincidence—your wife's name is Ann. What are the chances? You open the message and begin reading:

Ann, my love, it's me, Ricardo. It has been too long, but I cannot stop thinking about you. I yearn to hold your soft skin and to stare into your deep brown eyes again. These Hawaiian nights are somehow cold without you. Please let me see you again. I—

You're not sure what the point of this message is. The author doesn't seem to be selling anything. No matter. You shrug your shoulders.

Turn to page 133.

Turning onto the empty residential street, you have no choice but to accept the inconvenient truth: you lost that battle. But as you slip on your brass-rimmed aviator sunglasses, you soon grin and nod, for you haven't lost the war. Just what exactly this war is, you're not certain. It's not a war on terror—you participated in that first hand and know exactly what that was about (actually you don't). Is it a war on time? Or just a war on cheap coffee? If it is the latter, then you can't say that you lost *that* battle. The *PREMIUM QUALITY* swill is no more. Your house has been vanquished of that evil.

Yet as you cruise down the wide and quiet suburban streets, you wonder if, perhaps, you are part of something much bigger. A war on the day-to-day. A war on banality. A war on complacency. A war on boredom.

The War on Boredom. A worthy cause, you think. Surely that would galvanize global support. But who is the Osama Bin Laden of Boredom? Who is the figurehead that can be taken out by an elite squadron of black-op soldiers in order to rid the world of such evil?

And then you think something terrible. Something terrifying.

What if *you* are that figurehead? What if you are the Bin Laden of Boredom? Really, when is the last time you did something exciting? When is the last time you did something different? It seems that all you do of late is obsess about the most trivial of things. You weren't always like this, were you? Surely not. So when did it change? When did you become so boring? How could you have gone from being an elite fighter pilot to this... Looking forward to nothing more than a cold can of 7-UP on a summer afternoon. Nervous about getting out of the house on time. Fretting over subpar coffee grounds in the house. Debating the merits of a nine-minute snooze. When your cell phone then rings, you realize that you've yet to change the ringtone to something besides the factory preset. You've had this phone for six months and you haven't changed a thing. What does *that* say about you? Aren't people supposed to personalize their phones? If one's ringtone is truly a reflection of one's soul, then what is this saying?

You're a default.

"Hey Ann," you say upon activating the speakerphone.

"Hey, would you mind picking up Emma from daycare after work? I've just found out that an old friend from college is in town for the evening on a layover so I'll be a little late. Is that okay?"

"Sure."

"*And could you pick up some milk on the way home, as well?*"

"Okay. Actually, Ann," you quickly add before she might hang up. "Can I ask you a question?"

"*Of course.*"

"Am I boring?"

She doesn't reply. You think you hear a sigh. And then: "*What?*"

"Be honest, Ann: Have I become boring?"

"*No, I guess not.*"

"Really?"

"*What brought this on?*"

"I don't know. I just got thinking."

She laughs. Or she scoffs. Or maybe just another sigh? You're really not sure—it's so hard to tell on a phone. Considering the improvements in television picture quality over the last thirty years it seems quite a travesty that the audio fidelity of telephone calls remains just a notch above a couple Styrofoam cups connected with string. "*No, you're not boring.*"

"You mean that?"

"*Sure.*"

"Thanks. That's what I needed to hear."

"*Okay, so I guess I'll see you later this evening. I might be a little late.*"

"Okay. Bye honey. Love you." You say, but then realize that she'd already hung up. But no matter. Your sense of self worth has been restored, much like how the Afghani people will soon feel upon the triumphant conclusion of Operation Enduring Freedom (although you always preferred its more punchy original title, Operation Infinite Justice). You're not boring. You're a pilot! You were one of the elite, among the most skilled and respected (if not feared) fighter pilots in the American air force. You were—scratch that—you *are* the Ace of Spades. The best of the best.

Yes, you are going to change your ringtone as soon as you get to the airport. Kenny Loggin's *Danger Zone*. Prove to the world that you've still got it. They have free wi-fi there, you're pretty sure.

The End

■　■　■

ABOUT THE AUTHORS

Rudolf Kerkhoven lives a boring life with his wife and two kids in the Vancouver area of British Columbia. Daniel Pitts lives a boring life with wife and two kids in Calgary, Alberta.

www.RudolfKerkhoven.com

@BownessBooks

Made in the USA
Las Vegas, NV
15 February 2024

85848400R10083